Penguin Boo

NEW

NEW

Tales of the Unexpected

Penguin Books

PENGUIN BOOKS

Published by the Penguin Group
27 Wrights Lane, London W8 5TZ, England
Viking Penguin Inc., 40 West 23rd Street, New York, New York 10010, USA
Penguin Books Australia Ltd, Ringwood, Victoria, Australia
Penguin Books Canada Ltd, 2801 John Street, Markham, Ontario, Canada L3R 1B4
Penguin Books (NZ) Ltd, 182–190 Wairau Road, Auckland 10, New Zealand

Penguin Books Ltd, Registered Offices: Harmondsworth, Middlesex, England

This selection first published 1988
Reprinted 1988

This selection copyright © Anglia Television Ltd, 1988
All rights reserved

The acknowledgements on page 7 constitute an extension of this copyright page.

Made and printed in Great Britain by
Richard Clay Ltd, Bungay, Suffolk
Filmset in Monophoto Times

Contents

Acknowledgements   7

The Finger of Suspicion   Tony Wilmot   9

The Dead Don't Steal   Ella Griffiths (translated
   from the Norwegian by J. Basil Cowlishaw)   19

A Time to Die   Aileen Wheeler   28

Skeleton in the Cupboard   Tony Wilmot   34

Mr Know-All   W. Somerset Maugham   45

The Colonel's Lady   W. Somerset Maugham   53

Wink Three Times   John Charters   74

The Verger   W. Somerset Maugham   85

Acknowledgements

For permission to print the stories in this collection we are indebted to:

Tony Wilmot for 'The Finger of Suspicion', copyright © Tony Wilmot, 1985 (first published in *Weekend Extra*), and for 'Skeleton in the Cupboard', copyright © Tony Wilmot, 1983 (first published in *Weekend Extra*); Ella Griffiths and Laurence Pollinger Ltd for 'The Dead Don't Steal', copyright © Ella Griffiths, 1984, translation copyright © J. Basil Cowlishaw, 1986 (first published in *A-Magasinet*, Oslo, 17 November 1984); Aileen Wheeler for 'A Time to Die', copyright © Aileen Wheeler, 1987; A. P. Watt Ltd on behalf of The Royal Literary Fund and William Heinemann Ltd for W. Somerset Maugham's 'Mr Know-All' and 'The Verger' (from *The Collected Stories of W. Somerset Maugham*) and for 'The Colonel's Lady' (first published in *Creatures of Circumstances*, 1947); John Charters and Elspeth Cochrane Agency for 'Wink Three Times', copyright © John Charters, 1987.

The Finger of Suspicion

Tony Wilmot

The drab, sparsely furnished room was like every other police 'interview' room Tom had known: desk, half a dozen chairs, water-cooler and a telephone. Its sparseness was calculated; its purpose to intimidate a suspect, then to break him. A Y-shaped fan turned slowly overhead, barely moving the stale air. How many poor unfortunates, Tom wondered, had had their last breath of liberty in there?

It was 10 a.m. Already the desert sun's rays, piercing through the window blind, made Tom uncomfortably hot. The heat in the Persian Gulf was something he had never completely adapted to.

Two plain-clothes men, jackets off, shirts open, sat behind the desk. One invited Tom to sit. The man's voice was pure Harvard. Late twenties, Tom judged. Ruthless ambition personified. The other man had heavy jowls, gimlet eyes and a world-weary expression. Less ambitious, Tom decided, but just as ruthless.

Tom rested his hands on his knees, hoping he looked at ease. The local Arab police had arrested him the night before. They had been most apologetic. It wasn't their doing, they'd said – an extradition order from the USA. They had no choice but to comply with it.

In his mind's eye, Tom could see Soraya's worried expression as she had answered the doorbell in the small hours: an Arab inspector and a constable. *Tom, you promised me you'd given up your old way of life.* Tom had kept his promise; she must believe that. *Then what do the police want with you, Tom?*

Nothing, he'd said; obviously it was a mistake. They were confusing him with someone else. Anything to reassure her and give himself time to think. *But why do they talk of extradition? Doesn't that mean you will have to go back to America?* Tom didn't have a convincing answer to that.

The local police chief withdrew, closing the door as he left. Heavy-jowls opened a dossier on the desk-top and began to read aloud.

'Thomas Bradley, aged thirty-two, born Hartford, Connecticut . . .' He went on to list Tom's various employments since quitting high school, ending with '. . . last known occupation, chauffeur. Right so far, Bradley?'

Tom nodded. Let them do all the talking.

'What isn't included in your personal file, Bradley, are your, shall we say, extra-curricular activities – such as your penchant for petty larceny . . .'

The word 'penchant' caught Tom's attention. An odd word for a tough, world-weary FBI man to be using. Deep down, he'd always been expecting the FBI to catch up with him. He'd never confided that to Soraya; she would have only worried herself sick. And even if she suspected there were things in his past he would sooner forget about, she had never said.

Something else was bothering Tom. The way Heavy-jowls's sidekick was listening, observing, making mental notes. There was something about the man that was very un-cop like, more like a psychologist.

The grilling went on. Tom answered obliquely. Why volunteer information? But as the minutes slipped by Tom became more uneasy; their method of questioning was like nothing he'd known before – elliptic and full of subtle innuendo.

Suddenly the younger one said, 'You think we're *cops*, Bradley?' He made it sound like a four-letter word.

'Well, aren't you?' Tom felt cold inside . . . the Harvard accent, their unorthodox style, their beautifully tailored suits . . . the pieces were beginning to fall into place.

'We're not Police Department amateurs, Bradley. We're CIA.'

Tom had been 'into' petty larceny from leaving high school until his mid-twenties. The police had pulled him in a few times but could never get enough evidence to make a charge stick, releasing him with the usual veiled threats. He had been lucky. But he knew it was only a matter of time before they did nail him, so he decided to go straight. After a year or two, the police lost interest in him.

Tom took a training course as a chauffeur. He had always been able to handle a car well and he had the clean-cut looks that went with the uniform.

His first employment was as driver to the owner of a computer hardware firm. The man lived on Long Island. Tom found the work enjoyable, but the man's wife, riddled with complexes over having been born in the Bronx, was a pain – forever ordering him to drive her to Bloomingdale's or Macy's; forever castigating him for 'dumb insolence', for 'getting us into traffic snarl-ups', for 'not treating me like a lady'.

His patience finally snapped – and he quit. The computer man was sorry to lose him and gave him a glowing reference.

He had had a string of jobs after that. Then, one day, he got a call from his old boss, the computer man. A friend, government brass in Washington, was looking for a chauffeur. Was Tom available?

Tom made a favourable impression on the Washington man, a Mr Brodie, who said he would be in touch, but Tom heard nothing for a month. Then Mr Brodie's secretary rang: could Tom come in for a final interview?

Mr Brodie had looked distinctly embarrassed, Tom thought. He explained that something had been bothering him; perhaps Tom could straighten things out? A security check had revealed that Tom had once been under suspicion with the New York PD in connection with some robberies.

Tom had lied through his teeth. Not only had he not had anything to do with the crimes, he assured Mr Brodie, but he had filed a complaint for wrongful arrest and police harassment (he hadn't, but he knew it would be impossible for the N Y P D to refute it).

Mr Brodie had been all smiles. He had been sure that the answer would be no, but he had had to hear it from Tom's own lips. Now, how soon could Tom start?

Mr Brodie had an office in the National Security Agency. Everyone, even the senior staff, was on Christian-name terms. Tom was surprised at the informality – 'But it must always be "Sir" when we're outside the office, Tom' – but liked the atmosphere. The work was not too taxing and Mr Brodie was a pleasant man, easy to get along with. It was not long before Tom discovered that Brodie was cheating on his wife; but Tom decided it was no concern of his.

For months, the chauffeuring went smoothly. Then, off duty, Tom met a stunning girl in a singles bar. Her name was Charlene. Twenty-eight, a failed actress, a failed wife, she was determined to make a financial killing before she lost her looks.

She regarded Tom as a one-night stand – until she learned who he was working for. She had a mental file on every V I P in Washington. In her book, Brodie was *hot property*; somebody who handled top-secret data.

She had an apartment big enough for two, so why didn't Tom move in with her? (Tom couldn't move out of his rat-trap room fast enough!)

Night after night, the post-coital pillow-talk came around to the same theme: *Tom* had access to classified data . . . *Charlene* had access to a buyer . . .

'You listening to us, Bradley?'

Tom's thoughts were jerked back to the present.

The Harvard-voiced sidekick went on, 'You've got a cosy set-up here, Bradley. Shacked up with one of the local oil sheikh's wives. Risky, pal, risky. They're pretty severe on adultery here, aren't they? You and she could get fifty lashes for that.'

'The sheikh divorced her,' Tom said. 'We're married now.'

The sidekick laughed softly; even his laugh had a Harvard sound. 'Well, the honeymoon, as they say, is over. You'll be flying back to the States with us just as soon as the extradition papers are ready.' He paused. 'Does your new wife know you turned traitor, Bradley? No, I guess she doesn't. Couldn't bring yourself to tell her. Can't say I blame you. I'd be the same. It's a hell of an admission.'

Icy ripples ran up Tom's spine. He felt numb with shock. They must have broken Charlene. How else could they have found out?

'Know what puzzles *me*, Bradley?' said Heavy-jowls, who had identified himself as Powers. 'You could have gone to South America ... the Islands ... the South of France ... Australia. Yet you chose this Middle Eastern oil state. A place that's *dry*, for God's sake!'

Tom's reason had been blind panic. He had never experienced real fear before. Everything had suddenly crowded in on him. He had not been able to eat or sleep or think.

In the beginning getting data out of Mr Brodie's office had been something of a caper. Tom had read spy stories, and had always expected the real thing to be so much more difficult. But it could not have been easier. Files labelled *Top Secret* or *Confidential* were left lying around the office; and, often, when Mr Brodie was in meetings and Tom was waiting in the Cadillac outside, Tom could read defence memoranda in Mr Brodie's many briefcases, as often as not left unlocked.

Charlene had bought a micro-camera for him to use in Mr Brodie's office, but, crazily, he never needed it. All he had to do was photocopy the papers when Mr Brodie's secretary was out to lunch. The camera would have shown up on the personnel body scan, but the papers, hidden under his shirt, didn't.

It was all so simple. Charlene passed the info on to her contact (Tom never asked his nationality, preferring not to have his suspicions confirmed) and the money flowed in. Within a few months Tom's share amounted to 10,000 dollars.

Tom had wanted to stop then, to quit while they were ahead, but Charlene would not hear of it. To her, they had only scratched the surface.

Her contact was willing to pay 20,000 dollars for a copy of a file containing NATO intelligence-gathering activities. If Tom pulled that one off, *then* he could quit.

Weeks passed but Tom never even saw the file. He began to doubt its existence. Perhaps Mr Brodie was not as top-level as they thought, Tom suggested when Charlene's patience finally ran out.

It was the first time she ever threatened him. He'd better lay his hands on that file – or else! Or else what, Tom wanted to know. Would Charlene be ruthless enough to betray him?

He decided she probably would.

He renewed his efforts, rifling through Mr Brodie's briefcases at every opportunity. He found nothing that mentioned NATO's intelligence network.

Then, unexpectedly, Mr Brodie called him up to the office one morning and handed him some files from the safe to take down to the car. In a cellophane folder Tom saw what he had been looking for. He felt sick with excitement. He knew Mr Brodie trusted him implicitly; now he could use that trust like a tool.

Tom's instructions were to drive his boss to his home near Annapolis, first stopping at an address on the outskirts of Washington – Mr Brodie's mistress's apartment. (Two afternoons a week Tom would drop his boss off there, find a parking spot a few blocks away and read the paper for an hour before returning.)

He watched Mr Brodie disappear into the apartment block, then drove to a nearby shopping mall. He left his chauffeur's jacket and cap in the car, changed some dollar bills, then went to the public library. It took him exactly ten minutes to photocopy the file, page by page. He hid the copies under the plastic lining of the boot of the car.

And on the hour Tom – the likeable, good-looking, utterly trustworthy Thomas Bradley – drove back to collect Mr Brodie.

But Tom's euphoria was short-lived. Their buyer wanted to talk to Tom, to reassure himself that the file copies were genuine. Tom thought it too risky, but Charlene was insistent. He must talk to the man or the deal was off.

For two nights he didn't sleep. Matters came to a head when Charlene told him, 'Either you see him with me, Tom, or we're finished. And by that I mean *finished*. Period. I'll blow the whistle on you so loud it'll be like Watergate all over again.'

Tom would never have known the man was not American-born. Accent, mode of speech, behaviour, sense of humour – all were pure American. And all the time they talked, in an unfashionable bar, Tom never once felt like a traitor. Why, the guy could have been a family friend.

It was only later, in the cold light of day, that he realized he was in deep water. If a security leak were discovered, wouldn't he be the obvious suspect?

In a blind panic, he had drawn out his savings and flown to London. From there to Kuwait. Nobody would think of looking for him on the Persian Gulf, he knew. He could pose as an American oil technician until he found work. But as he drifted from one oil state to another, his dollars had melted at an alarming rate. That was when he met Soraya. She hired him as her chauffeur-bodyguard, and very soon had extended his duties in a most delightful way.

*

Powers lit a cigarette and leaned back in his chair. He tapped the dossier with a well-manicured fingernail.

'It says here, Bradley, that you run a small nightclub . . .'

'Yes,' Tom said. 'I gave up the chauffeur's job six months back.'

'Sheikh catch you on the back seat with another of his wives?'

The sidekick laughed; it was more a snicker than a laugh.

Tom said nothing. The club had been Soraya's idea; she had once been the sheikh's favourite belly-dancer. The place was beginning to show a modest profit.

'When will I be flown back?' Tom asked.

'First plane tomorrow.'

'What will I get for this?' Tom added. 'Life imprisonment?'

Neither CIA man said anything for a while. Then Powers closed the dossier. 'That's the normal sentence. But there's an irony about your case, Bradley. You see, all that stuff you and your fancy woman sold was worthless. Pure garbage. Dreamed up by my department.'

Powers spoke slowly, relishing every word. The CIA had long suspected a Russian sleeper was operating in Washington. So when they realized Tom was stealing information from Brodie's office, they had allowed it to continue in the hope of smoking the agent out. And it had worked. The only thing they hadn't expected was for Tom to skip the country.

'Don't *you* find that ironic, Bradley? That the Ruskie was paying good money for trash? And you were the dupe?'

They laughed.

Tom tried to join in, but his lips felt frozen. He was on the receiving end of the much-talked-about dirty-tricks department. No wonder all those confidential files had been left lying around Mr Brodie's office! They had been an *invitation*.

'But that doesn't let *you* off the hook, Bradley,' Powers went on, watching the overhead fan carve into a smoke ring, 'Oh no, pal. *You* didn't know the stuff you were selling wasn't your government's secrets. So you're going to be charged as a Grade One Spy, Bradley. And that will certainly mean life.'

Once again Tom sat, stony-faced, as the CIA men chuckled.

Powers became expansive. 'Make it easier on yourself, Bradley. The CIA has influence. Make a full confession now, and we'll do everything we can to help. Do you read me?'

Perfectly, Tom thought. It was a crude attempt at plea bargaining. And did he detect a note of desperation in Powers's voice?

'That NATO file was printed on specially treated paper, Bradley. Every one of its pages has a full set of finger and thumb prints of your left hand. We simply compare *your* prints with those on the file ... and you're sunk. The judge will almost certainly hand out the maximum sentence ...'

As Powers's voice went on, turning the screw tighter, Tom's thoughts flew back. He had worn his chauffeur's gloves at the library's photocopier. But he had taken off his left glove to be able to turn the pages more quickly.

As evidence in court, it would be damning; but it didn't matter now. These two CIA hatchet-men didn't know it yet, but he was going to walk out of the room a free man.

'You haven't got a case against me.' He spoke softly but firmly. '*You can't compare my prints.*'

'Is this your idea of a joke, Bradley?' Powers said.

Tom smiled grimly. 'You could say that. And the joke's on both of us.'

He raised his left hand, slowly, and placed it on the desk-top. The fingers and thumb had an unnatural smoothness.

The next morning, as Soraya lay sleeping, Tom watched the dawn break from their balcony. He watched the sun rise above minarets and terracotta roof-tops, framed by the huge dome of the mosque. Soon the bell would sound the call for Islamic prayer. The town would come alive. A new day would begin.

Tom faced himself honestly. He had not been happy about

17

selling his country's secrets – but he was weak. He had never been able to resist the temptation of easy money. It made it easier to live with his conscience, now, knowing that he had not really passed on anything useful to the Soviet agent. And there was a curious irony in that he had helped the CIA – albeit unknowingly – to nail the man.

Overhead Tom heard the whine of jet engines as they hauled their pay-load into the crystal-clear dawn sky. The London plane. The two CIA men would be on it, on the first leg of their trip back to the States.

He smiled. Would he ever forget the looks on their faces when he explained why he had had to give up his job as a chauffeur?

There had been a charity ball, six months earlier, organized by the wives of the local oil tycoons. Tom had never seen so much jewellery on display in any one place before. It stirred up all his old criminal instincts. Besides, jewellery was easy to transport and no problem to fence.

But the months of soft living with Soraya had dulled his reflexes. He had allowed himself to get caught with a pocketful of diamond necklaces.

Tom had discovered that Islamic law did not discriminate in favour of foreigners; that it dealt harshly with thieves. Very harshly.

He stared at the appendage strapped on to the end of his left forearm. He had hated the sight of the thing at first; now he was beginning to think of it as a part of himself.

His physiotherapist would be arriving soon, with a new set of exercises. The physiotherapist thought Tom might soon be able to drive a car again. Of course, he reflected, it would never have the same dexterity as a real hand. But it was a thousand times better than no hand at all.

The Dead Don't Steal

Ella Griffiths
Translated from the Norwegian by J. Basil Cowlishaw

The ringing of the phone on his desk brought Curt Lessner's head up with a jerk. Every time it rang he was afraid it was the police.

This time it was – the Traffic Division.

'Morning, Mr Lessner,' a friendly Bergen voice said. 'Inspector Svendsen here. We've found your car. At least, our friends across the border have. Found it in Arvika – double-parked outside a supermarket. Double-parked and with a lady's handbag on the seat. Full of the usual junk, you know – powder compact, comb, all that sort of stuff. Driving licence, too. *And* a couple of credit cards. Shouldn't take long to trace who owns it. One of my lads is on to it now.'

A feeble 'Oh?' was all Lessner was able to manage before the inspector went on: 'The Swedes drove your car to the border and we picked it up there. The forensic boys'll have to give it a good going-over first – prints, you know, things like that – then you can have it back. It's all in one piece, so don't worry.'

'Well, thank you,' Curt Lessner said, clearing his throat. 'Strange that someone should leave a handbag in it, though, isn't it?' he ventured.

'The woman who took your car did more than leave her bag behind,' Inspector Svendsen answered. 'On the way to Arvika she stopped at a café. Anders', it's called. Just the other side of the border. Had a snack. Well, a dinner, actually. Meat and veg and all the trimmings. Anyway, somehow she managed to break a sauceboat. Sauce all over the place, the manager said. Most of it went on to the sofa, I gather. Nothing on her,

19

apparently. The manager took it in his stride, but she was awfully put out, it seems – wanted to pay for the damage and getting the sofa cleaned. In the end she left her card so that they could contact her when they knew what it came to. So there you are: we've had it handed to us on a plate, so to speak.' The inspector laughed heartily at his own joke.

'But how did you find all this out so quickly?' Lessner asked. 'That she'd stopped at a café, I mean.'

'Simple. The bill from Anders' was in her bag. Dated the same day. The Swedish police checked with the café, and there you are.'

'But if you know that much, then you must know her name as well. I mean to say, driving licence and all that . . .'

'Of course we do,' the policeman agreed. 'It's no secret. Lillen Aas. Lillen Johanne Aas, to be exact. Lives in Skippergaten, out at Nordstrand. Number twenty-two. Three-roomed flat. Very nice too, I hear. Not my department, actually, but I sent one of our cars up to have a look. There was no one home. Never mind, she's bound to turn up soon. And when she does we'll let you know.'

'Lillen Aas?' Curt Lessner stammered. 'But she's my secretary! She's been off work for a few days – since Monday, in fact. But it's only been two days since my car disappeared . . .'

'Nothing very strange about that,' said the inspector. 'She could have taken your car without showing up for work, couldn't she? Did you ever lend it to her, by the way?'

'Yes, sometimes. Odd errands for the office, you know.'

'Will you be wanting to take the matter further, Mr Lessner?' the inspector asked. 'Prosecute, that is.'

'Er, er . . . I don't know.' Lessner made an effort to pull himself together. 'I suppose I ought to, really. But Lillen . . . Do I have to decide that now?' he asked.

'No, Mr Lessner,' the inspector reassured him. 'There's plenty of time for that.'

Curt Lessner thanked him and put the phone down. His

mind reeling, he buried his face in his hands. Lillen – Lill – couldn't possibly have stolen his car. Nor could she have broken a sauceboat in a café in Sweden.

People who're dead don't steal cars. They don't steal anything.

And Lillen Aas *was* dead.

He'd killed her himself.

Everything had gone so well until Lill entered his life.

Blonde, petite, with eyes of speedwell blue, one day she had walked blithely into his office to apply for the vacant post of secretary in the small charter business and travel agency he had opened barely three years earlier.

'I haven't many references, I'm afraid,' she'd said with a disarming smile. 'On the other hand I learn fast.'

She was twenty-six. A woman, but a woman who, outwardly at least, had somehow retained the naïveté of a child.

'Can you type?'

'Yes. Not all that fast, but I'm pretty accurate. I have it taped, in other words.'

'"Taped"?' he'd mused. Strange expression for a girl as young as she was to use.

Later he had come to realize that she was full of contradictions like that.

She was right about learning fast.

She did. Very fast.

Annie hadn't liked her at all – understandably. Having been married to her Curt for twenty-odd years, she soon tumbled to the fact that he was up to something. Or, rather, that *they* were. And she'd been right. Only three nights later he and his new secretary found themselves in bed together.

After that there was no going back, at least not for him.

He had misjudged her completely. Taken it for granted that she'd jump at a chance to get into the racket. Earn a small fortune and then perhaps in a few years, when they'd stashed enough away, decamp to the Caribbean. Both of them. Settle down and enjoy life in a country where prices were more reasonable than in Norway and where a person could bask in the sunshine all year round instead of spending half the time frozen to the marrow. The plan was simplicity itself. All she had to do was to act as a courier. Take parties of tourists over, show them around, and bring them back. Only in her luggage on the return trip there was always a wad or two of brightly coloured tourist brochures, tightly held by elastic bands. Nothing strange about that. If she were ever asked, she had only to say that they needed them to help make brochures of their own in Norwegian. But she never *was* asked – which was just as well, since a small space cut out in the middle of each bundle was packed tight with cocaine.

After three trips Lill had suddenly called a halt. She wanted out. She had earned enough to make her comfortable, and what was more, she had fallen for one of the pilots on the Rio run. So that was that.

'But what about me?' he'd protested, his whole world suddenly shattered.

'You? You'll be all right. You're not exactly short of money, are you? And as for you-know-what, well – you have your Annie. You *are* married, you know. Besides, you're twenty years older than I am, don't forget. Twenty. That's eighteen too many as far as I'm concerned.'

If only she'd not brought up the difference in their ages! Or not smiled so ... condescendingly. Pityingly, almost. She'd made him feel practically senile.

That was why he'd killed her. Not that he'd meant to.

Before he realized it he'd lashed out at her and caught her a glancing blow behind the ear with the flat of his hand. It had sent her reeling, and as she fell her head struck the corner of his desk with a dull thud. Even now he wasn't sure whether it was he or the desk that had killed her. What he did know was that she was undeniably dead. She'd just crumpled up on the floor and lain staring up at him with sightless blue eyes until finally, unable to bear it any longer, he'd steeled himself to close them.

Aghast at what he'd done, he'd sat down for a moment to consider his next move. Strangely enough, there didn't seem to be any blood, and it was that that had encouraged him to try to get away with it. The point was: how?

Obviously he had to get the body out of his office without being seen. Now, right away. It was already getting late – which fortunately meant that it was dark.

That was probably why he'd managed it.

But *had* he managed it? It was all beginning to seem unreal.

After the inspector's phone call he sat quietly for a while, trying to steady his nerves. Then he locked up the office and drove home in the car he'd hired in place of his own. As soon as he got in he strode across to the drinks cabinet in the living-room and poured himself a stiff measure of whisky. Gulping it down almost in one, he seated himself at the window and stared out into the night.

Before him lay the garden, but all he saw was the place where Lill's body lay, deep in some undergrowth, well off the beaten track.

'What's wrong, Curt?' his wife asked sharply, entering the room from the kitchen. 'You've been acting so strangely lately. What's got into you?'

'The police phoned,' he answered, his face averted. 'Just before I left. They've found the car. Across the border in Arvika. Lillen's handbag was on the seat. There were some other things, too . . .'

'That hussy!' his wife burst out. 'A hussy and a thief, that's what she is! It doesn't surprise me in the least. I've known it all along. Well, it'll put a stop to your fun and games, that's one good thing.'

23

'Don't talk like that, Annie,' her husband said thickly. 'There's never been anything between us. I've told you so before. All I've ever done is to defend her when you kept on running her down. Anyway, I don't think *she* took the car. More likely someone else who wanted to hurt her for some reason.'

'There you go again, defending her! If she didn't steal the car, why hasn't she shown a sign of life? Reported her handbag missing? She's bound to have had something in it more important than a compact and a lipstick. Women always do these days. Credit cards, that kind of thing. Oh, no, this time she's gone too far! Just wait till I see her again, I'll tell her a thing or two, believe you me! She can't twist *me* round her little finger, the way she can you.'

Curt Lessner looked at his wife without answering. Suddenly he rose to his feet and stumbled to the bathroom. He reached it just in time to be sick into the wash-basin.

He knew Lill was dead. And the dead don't steal.

Or break sauceboats.

Later that night he was taken really ill. He felt feverish and several times he found himself in the bathroom again, trying to be sick. Only now the sole result was a heaving stomach and a dry rasp in his throat.

'You can't go on like this, Curt,' his wife said. 'We shall have to get the doctor.' They were the first kind words she'd spoken to him for a long time, he reflected sadly. Ever since Lillen Aas had come into his life, in fact.

'It'll pass,' he assured her. 'I'll be all right in the morning, you'll see. I must have had something that's disagreed with me.'

His wife gave him a searching look but held her peace.

As he lay tossing and turning, unable to sleep, he realized that she too was still awake. His brain was in a whirl. What on earth was he to do? He was certain that Lill was dead. But dead people didn't steal cars, he reasoned yet again. Or spill sauce on sofas . . .

Shortly before nine next morning he phoned the inspector and told him – which was true enough – that he thought the whole story of the car theft had something fishy about it. 'Why should she leave her bag on the seat?' he asked. 'And how did she come to break a sauceboat? Sounds crazy to me. Do you have a description of her? The people at the café must remember what she looked like.'

'All I know is that she was blonde and looked very young. Childlike, the manager said. But I can phone the police in Arvika and ask if they know any more, if you like,' the policeman offered.

'No, don't bother,' Curt Lessner said hastily. 'There's no need for that. It's just that it all seems so strange to me. I mean, she only had to ask me and I'd have let her have the car anyway. She must have known that . . .'

'Just a moment,' the inspector broke in. 'Hang on a sec, will you?' Curt Lessner heard him lay the receiver aside and walk away. A minute or so later he returned and said: 'It seems that the car was full of Lillen Johanne Aas's finger prints. So there we are – it must have been her who drove it to Arvika.'

'Oh, well – yes, I see. That settles it, then, doesn't it?' Curt Lessner said lamely, hurrying to replace the receiver before it fell from his hand.

While he was shaving he studied his face in the mirror. 'God,' he thought to himself, 'I look like death warmed up.' He shuddered as the grotesque aptness of the expression suddenly struck him. At breakfast he gave up after a tentative bite of toast.

'Stay at home, Curt,' his wife urged him. 'You can't go to the office in that state. It's Saturday, anyway. And I'd be a darned sight happier if you'd let the doctor have a look at you.'

'Nonsense,' her husband replied irritably. 'Of course I'm going. Place doesn't run itself, you know.'

He changed his mind, however, when he realized that Annie was going into town. If he really had been having hallucinations, he had better find out straightaway. And the only way to do that was to go back to where he had hidden Lill's body and make sure.

If only none of it had ever happened! 'Oh, God,' he thought to himself, 'let it all be in my mind!' But somehow he knew that it wasn't.

He felt he would give anything to be able to see Lill again. Just to see her – alive! She could marry anyone she liked. He'd never trouble her again. No other woman, either. He'd learnt his lesson. Dear, dear Lill ...

As soon as his wife was safely out of the house he took the hire car and drove the same route he had taken on that fateful night with Lill's body lying crumpled up under a blanket on the back seat. Her last drive. It *must* have been.

He stopped the car at the same place as last time. Nerving himself, he opened the door and half-walked, half-ran to the thicket into which he had thrust the body.

Stumbling into the midst of it, he parted the bushes and peered into the shadows. The body was exactly where he had left it.

At that moment he heard the sound of footsteps crashing through the bushes behind him.

It was the police.

First to arrive on the scene was Inspector Svendsen, the policeman he'd spoken to on the phone. Just behind him Curt Lessner glimpsed the trim figure of a woman. The inspector introduced her: Detective Sergeant Sylvia Larsgaard.

'I realized as soon as Lill disappeared that something serious must have happened to her. She loved that flat of hers. It was almost a part of her. She'd never have gone off and left it like that. She told me once that she knew something about you that could ruin you for life, only she never said what it was. As the days went by, I got to thinking about what she'd said. That's what made me take your car. I thought that if you'd killed her and I could fix it so that it seemed she was still alive – well, with a bit of luck you'd feel you had to go back and see. She had the other key, remember? I found it on her dressing-table. And – well, it worked, didn't it?'

Detective Sergeant Sylvia Larsgaard. Blonde, petite, eyes like speedwells. Four or five years older than Lill, but even so the very image of her sister.

A Time to Die

Aileen Wheeler

Ellison Liddell was a self-made man and inordinately proud of his handiwork.

Born into a large family of humble parentage, he had soon shaken off his working-class origins and by single-minded deployment of his considerable abilities in the field of electronics, his innovative talent, capacity for hard work and sheer ruthlessness in the removal of all obstacles, he had, in his late forties, acquired very healthy business interests, a large, imposing, exquisitely furnished house, expensive cars, holiday properties overseas and not one financial cloud in his successful sky. Most men in his position would have been content to rest upon their laurels. Not so Ellison.

He had enjoyed accumulating his wealth; now he aspired to two more of life's glittering prizes – an honour of some sort and an heir. The stumbling block to both these ambitions lay in the person of his wife, Dulcie.

Recently, he had spent much time painstakingly cultivating the 'right' people and, although normally careful with money, had begun giving largely to worthy causes, pretending dismay when the news of his 'secret' generosity was carefully leaked.

Unfortunately, Dulcie did not share his social aspirations, proving, in fact, a distinct embarrassment to them, so, with the ruthless efficiency that characterized all his enterprises, he decided to dispose of her, completely and soon. She was too old, anyway, to provide him with the son he so desired and now that he had met Violette, a lovely, thirty-year-old French woman, widow of a former business competitor, he knew he had found the perfect partner. Wealthy in her own right, she possessed the looks, breeding and business acumen that made her infinitely attractive in his eyes. What a hostess she would make! What a fitting mother of his children! He sensed also, correctly, that she was equally attracted to him, for he had retained his early good looks and was not without a certain facile charm. Only dull, dreary little Dulcie stood between him and the perfect marriage. Dulcie was a drag. Dulcie must go.

She had not always been so dispensable. When they had married, almost twenty-five years earlier, he had been merely Leslie Sydney Norman – L. S. N. – Liddle, possessed of nothing but burning ambition. Frustrated, he had soon learned that ambition alone was insufficient for rapid advancement unless backed by funds. How could one accumulate unless able to speculate? Dulcie had entered his life, a plain, homely, guileless girl of his own age, and had fallen hopelessly in love with him. At first, her affections were completely unrequited, but when her widowed mother died suddenly, leaving to her only child a comfortable semi-detached house, a tidy sum of money and the benefits of a substantial insurance policy, the young Liddle had considered it his moral duty to protect the poor, motherless girl from fortune hunters. He had swept her into marriage, inveigled her into putting all her worldly goods into their joint names, founded his own business and after changing his name to the more impressive sounding Ellison Liddell, had hitched his wagon to the star of success.

At first, Dulcie had been blissfully happy, but as their standard of living escalated, she found herself unable to keep pace, her own ambition extending no farther than 'a nice new three-piece suite and some cosy velvet curtains for the winter'. When Ellison decided they should move from their modest little home to something more imposing, she had been heart-broken.

As the years passed she found herself increasingly out of her social depth, quite unable to adapt to her husband's opulent lifestyle. Starved of affection and understanding, she turned, as do so many emotionally deprived people, to food and drink for comfort, sweet, sugary things affording her particular consolation. In consequence, she gained weight alarmingly, soon looking years older than Ellison, who had taken great care of his appearance. Miserably depressed by this, she sought solace in yet greater quantities of tempting delicacies.

In the early days of their marriage it had been Dulcie who had wanted children, but Ellison had decided firmly against it, for no domestic distractions were to be allowed to come between him and his goals. Now, however, he decided the time had come to found a Liddell dynasty and, as usual when he made a decision, he intended wasting no time in implementing it.

Things would, of course, be so much easier could he simply divorce Dulcie, pensioning her off into a saccharine world of endless cream cakes, syrupy drinks and the romantic novelettes to which she was addicted. However, in the early days it had been expedient to tie her into the business, at least nominally, for tax purposes, and so intricately was she woven in that even she had no idea how much power she possessed, at least on paper; to divest her of that power now would be to reduce his own financial assets considerably.

Another important factor was that Violette hailed from an aristocratic, if impecunious, French Catholic family – another of her attractions – and would never consider allying herself to a man with a wife still living. So what alternative was there? Dulcie must invest him with the dignity of a widower.

With the characteristic meticulousness of a man who had never yet put a foot wrong, he began planning Dulcie's demise with infinite care, drawing upon his expert electronic skills.

First, he must implant in Dulcie's mind the idea that there was a gas leak in the house; like most compliant people, she was very suggestible and would be sure to have the Gas Board check this out thoroughly. Nevertheless, the seeds of suspicion would be sown.

Then, on a carefully chosen day when he could be sure of Dulcie's absence from home, he would install a small but highly concentrated explosive charge to the gas meter, connect a timing device to the clock of the central heating system, set the fuse to detonate at eleven o'clock that night, it being Dulcie's invariable custom never to retire later than 10.15 p.m., and at the very moment that the house and contents were blasted to extinction, he, Ellison, would be establishing a nice, watertight alibi many miles away.

Naturally, the insurance people would leave no stone or piece of rubble unturned to ascertain the cause of the explosion, but they were not dealing with an incompetent amateur and he would make quite sure that nothing used could survive the holocaust, no tell-tale remains to point the finger of suspicion in his direction.

As always, he had a certain amount of luck, two factors in particular working to his advantage. A sinus disorder impaired Dulcie's sense of smell and it was simplicity itself convincing her of the presence of a strong odour of gas, which she speedily reported. A Gas Board inspector duly arrived, checked the system thoroughly and gave it a clean bill of health, but several times during the following weeks, Ellison succeeded in alarming her sufficiently so that she summoned the inspector three times more, until she became considered something of a crank. But to Dulcie, Ellison's word was law and if he smelled gas, then it must be the inspector who was in error. By now, she genuinely believed that she, too, could smell the leak and was constantly confiding her fears to Mrs Halliday, the daily help.

Ellison's second piece of luck came from Dulcie being a complete creature of habit. Always on Thursdays she visited her cousin Doris, who lived some ten miles distant, leaving home in her little car on the dot of ten in the morning and returning at precisely ten at night, when she would retire to bed with her hot chocolate, custard creams, sleeping pills and sentimental literature.

The opportunity to put his plan into action came when Ellison was invited to an important dinner to be held on a Thursday evening at an hotel in the next county. The conditions were ideal; even he couldn't have arranged them better.

Several times in the hearing of Mrs Halliday he tried to persuade Dulcie to accompany him, promising her an expensive new evening gown for the occasion. As he had been certain she would, Dulcie had declined, detesting social exposure and being unwilling to disappoint Doris. Mrs Halliday pursed her lips contemptuously. What a silly creature Mrs Liddell was. Catch her, Elsie Halliday, passing up a chance like that!

On the day of the dinner, a chill day in late November, Ellison returned from his office at the end of the afternoon to an empty house and began his preparations. All went smoothly but, being a perfectionist, he checked and double-checked, even confirming the exact time by the speaking clock before resetting the central heating control and switching it on again.

After dressing carefully, he took a last look around the house. It would all be gone when he returned. There was no sentimentality in him and he had few regrets at the prospect of its loss. Now was the time for new beginnings.

The dinner was a grand occasion, which normally he would have enjoyed to the full. Tonight, however, his mind returned repeatedly to the scene of his crime and at eleven o'clock he almost imagined that he heard the explosion, but he had always possessed nerve and nobody present suspected the inner tension and excitement simmering below the surface of his usual urbane manner.

At about twelve-fifty, he drove into the exclusive avenue where he lived, prepared for the chaotic scene that should await him. Fire engines, ambulances, police waiting to break the dire news, onlookers avid for sensation – all the confusion associated with the aftermath of disaster.

The avenue was completely quiet, the well-spaced, detached

houses slumbering peacefully beneath the cold, starry sky. His own house, in darkness, stood intact.

Inside, all was exactly as he had left it. Puzzled, he ran upstairs to Dulcie's room. It was empty, her bed not slept in. For the first time in his life, he felt totally disorientated. What possibly could have gone so wrong?

As he returned to the hall, the phone rang. It was Dulcie, apologizing for her absence and explaining that Doris had persuaded her to stay the night because of the power cut occurring just as she had been about to leave for home. Didn't he know about the power cut? It had affected an area for a radius of twenty miles and had lasted exactly two hours. She apologized again, promised she would be home in time to prepare his breakfast, said goodnight and hung up.

Ellison replaced the phone slowly. Power cut! Suddenly, the import of it dawned upon him. With mounting horror, he looked at the electric clock on the wall. The second hand was within moments of 11 p.m. He hurled himself in panic towards the front door, but too late. Just as he had so carefully planned, to the very last second, the house was blown to smithereens as the hands on the time switch reached eleven. Ellison Liddell had made the first – and last – miscalculation of his life.

Skeleton in the Cupboard

Tony Wilmot

He was watching the park gates from his usual bench by the pond. The girl would soon be joining him for her mid-day break.

For several days now they had sat at the same bench and exchanged pleasantries after she had laughed at the way the ducks fought over the crusts he had thrown to them.

She was twenty-ish, attractive, with a pulse-quickening figure, but he did not flatter himself that her interest was in any way sexual. He subscribed to the adage 'No fool like an old fool'. Besides, he was more than twice her age.

To him it was a harmless flirtation – a fillip to his middle-aged man's morale – and he had found himself looking forward to their lunchtime 'assignations'.

Earlier that morning, however, events had taken a more serious turn. The girl had paid a visit to the Vehicle Registration Department in the Town Hall.

His secretary had come into his office. 'There's a young lady here, Mr Smythe, asking if we keep records of car ownership . . . M G sports cars in particular. I said I thought not.'

He had felt a twinge of unease at the mention of the car type.

'Quite so,' he had replied. 'Tell her registrations are all on the national computer now. In any case, we couldn't give out that kind of information.'

He had peered at the reception desk through his office's glass partition. The enquirer was the girl from the park bench.

An odd coincidence, he had thought. Or was it something more?

Now, as she entered the park gates with that long stride and purposeful expression, his unease returned.

'Hello – we meet again,' she said, sitting beside him.

'Ah, yes . . . sky looks a bit overcast. Hope we aren't in for some rain.' He gestured at the apple she was peeling with a penknife. 'Lunch?'

'Yes, worse luck. I'm on a diet.'

He smiled. 'You seem to be here most days. Do you work hereabouts?'

'Oh no. In fact, I don't live here. I'm just staying in town while I'm doing some research. I'm from Elmston, actually.'

'Really? I know Elmston . . .' he began. The words were out before the warning bell rang. 'Well, I don't exactly know it . . . pal of mine . . . knew him years ago . . . used to live there. Is this your first visit here?'

'Yes.'

'Nice place,' he said. 'Bit dull, though.'

'Not at all. It's charming.'

'What are you researching? Our town's chequered history, perhaps? Parts date from the Roman occupation.'

'How interesting. But no – I'm trying to trace someone.'

'Ah! Bit of detective work?'

She smiled. 'In a way. I'm beginning to find out what a job it is tracing someone who may not want to be traced. No wonder the police have to spend so much time on investigations.'

'And the "trail" has led from Elmston to here?'

'Indirectly, yes. But I've had to spend time in several places first. I'm hoping this will be the last.'

'Sounds very intriguing,' he said, hoping to entice her to reveal more without seeming to be prying into her private life.

'I suppose it is, in a way. I'm going back more than twenty years, though.' She made a wry face. 'Which is setting myself a difficult task.'

'I don't suppose you were even born then?' he said.

'I was – just! Anyway, I've managed to unearth a few clues. The person I'm looking for had an M G sports car then and got married during the same period. I know it's a bit of a long shot, but it might just pay off.'

His unease became a shiver which set him on edge even more. He was like the rabbit hypnotized by the snake, wanting to get away but unable to move. 'But I mustn't bore you with my personal affairs,' she went on. 'What about you? What line of business are you in?'

'Oh, nothing much. Civil servant, actually. Quite dull, I'm afraid. I wish I could be an 007 like you but . . . I'm just a nine-to-five chap.'

'Don't be so modest. There's nothing wrong with being a civil servant.'

He made a deprecating gesture but inwardly he was thrilled that a pretty girl was finding him interesting enough to want to flirt with him.

'Married, of course?'

He was on the point of saying no when he noticed her glance at the ring on his left hand. He nodded.

'The dishy men always are! Lived here long, have you?'

He did not like the turn the conversation was taking. 'Oh, quite some time.' He made a show of checking his wristwatch. 'Well, I must be getting back. The grindstone waits for no man! I, er . . . that is, perhaps we might see each other again tomorrow?'

'Yes, let's. About one o'clock?'

He said that would be fine.

As he walked back to the Town Hall doubts and fears scurried around his head like cornered rats. It was just too damned close to be coincidence any more. For *he* used to run an M G. And *he* had married twenty years ago.

He could not concentrate at the office. An hour before finishing time, he got his car from the staff car-park and drove to his semi in a leafy suburb on the outskirts of town.

Margaret, his wife, was doing some work in the garden. 'Robert, is that you? You're early. Nothing wrong at the office, is there?'

'No, of course not.' Why did women always think the worst? 'I thought I'd finish off that lampstand in the shed while there's still some daylight.'

'Right-o! I'll call you when dinner's ready.'

He put the inside catch on the shed door and made sure his wife was still in the front garden. Then he got a metal box from behind his workbench.

The key to the box was hidden under a bottle of weedkiller. Inside the box were two yellowing clippings from the *Elmston Observer*.

One was headlined: *Girl, 10, killed in hit-and-run*.

For the umpteenth time he read how the girl had been knocked down on a pedestrian crossing while on her way home from a schoolfriend's house.

The details were embedded in his memory. He had driven over to Margaret's parents' house in the M G that evening. They had lived just outside Elmston then.

Because of some road works, the traffic had been diverted.

He had been exceeding the speed limit, too. It was an unfamiliar route and the crossing had taken him by surprise.

The car's brakes were slack because he'd skipped a service to save money, and a shower had made the road surface slippery . . .

Even though it was twenty years ago, he could still remember the sickening thud . . . the scream . . . the crumpled body on the side of the road.

Of course, he should have stopped, but he had panicked. He

had been short-listed for a new job for which a clean driving licence was a condition of employment and it was only days away from his wedding. Reporting the accident would have ruined everything.

The second clipping, headed *Police appeal for witnesses*, said several people had heard the screech of brakes but none had seen the accident.

A police spokesman was quoted as saying they were 'pursuing several lines of enquiry'.

He locked the clippings away again and returned the box to its hiding place. He had never fully understood why he had kept them all those years. What, he wondered, would the psychologists make of that? A guilt complex, perhaps? A subconscious desire to punish himself for his crime?

It was his favourite tuna-fish salad for dinner but the memory of the accident had dulled his appetite. He pecked away at it, nodding absently as Margaret related the events of her day.

All through the meal the thought kept hammering in his brain: how long before the girl found out that *he* was the hit-and-run driver?

More than likely she was a former schoolfriend wanting to see justice done. Or a relative ... the dead girl's sister, even.

The police enquiries had no doubt fizzled out years ago – they would have had far more pressing cases on their plate – but the little girl's family and friends would not have given up the search.

That night he hardly slept. At the office next day he clockwatched until it was time to go to the park. The girl was already there when he arrived.

'I was hoping I'd see you today,' she said. 'You see, I'm certain I've come to the right town. You know I mentioned an M G ... well, how's this for amateur sleuthing? ... There's the car's number.'

A muscle in his cheek began to twitch rapidly as he read what was in her notebook. *His* MG's number. But how had she . . .? The newspaper report said there had been no eye-witnesses.

'I'm missing the middle one or two digits in the number-plate – but it's enough.'

'Very cloak-and-daggerish,' he said, forcing a smile. 'Have you tried the local Vehicle Registration Department? Perhaps they can help.'

'Oh yes. No luck, though. But guess what – I've got a photograph of the car.'

The park seemed to spin. He gripped the bench with both hands.

'You all right?' she asked.

'What? Oh yes. Just a twinge of indigestion.'

'Well, I haven't actually got the photograph,' she went on. 'I've only seen the negative. I'm having a ten-by-eight print done from it.'

'You have been busy!' His voice sounded unreal. 'Look, that friend of mine from Elmston. I've just remembered. *He* had an MG. He could be who you are looking for . . . I might still have an address for him at home . . . Have you got a phone number where I can contact you? Better still, an address in case I miss you here tomorrow.'

She wrote down both in her notebook and tore the page out for him. 'Now I must be off,' she said. 'I've got more sleuthing to do. I'll look out for you here again tomorrow.'

He gave her a minute or two's start, then began to follow her.

Her first stop was at a photographic shop near the main square. She came out carrying a large buff-coloured en-velope.

That would be the MG print, he thought, as he observed her getting her bearings.

He kept about fifty yards behind as she crossed the town centre to the offices of the *Evening Gazette*.

39

He followed her through the revolving doors, keeping the public newspaper stands in the foyer between himself and the point where she was talking at the enquiry counter.

Pretending to leaf through the week's back numbers, he could hear snatches of conversation above the din of typewriters and telephones.

'. . . wedding report twenty-one years ago . . . would it be possible to . . .'

'. . . archives are on the fourth floor . . . first door on the right as you come out of the lift . . .'

He watched the girl take the lift. Time passed. People came and went. He felt clammy and conspicuous.

Eventually she reappeared out of the lift. The receptionist smiled. Had she found what she had been looking for?

Yes, she had.

He was in a cold sweat now, but he had no difficulty keeping her in sight, for he knew the town like the back of his hand. Where would she head next? Oh God, he thought, don't let it be the police station.

'Robert! Long time no see!' He started. It was a man he knew from the Parks Department. He felt like a schoolboy caught playing truant. 'Stretching your legs, eh, Robert?'

'Oh, er, yes.' He could see the girl disappearing down a side turning. 'Popped out for cigarettes.'

The man was grinning. 'Some looker, eh?'

'What?'

'That girl you were staring at.'

'Oh,' he forced a smile. 'Look, can't stop now. Let's have a drink next week. I'll ring you.'

When he finally got away, the girl was nowhere to be seen. He spent the rest of the afternoon fretting at his desk. Whose wedding had she looked up? And why?

It was not until he and Margaret were watching TV that evening that the answer came to him; in fact, it was staring him in the face . . .

On the piano was an ornately framed picture of him and Margaret on their wedding day. Of course! Why hadn't he thought of it sooner? The other photos in the family album: there was one of the MG.

He found the album and flicked through it. There it was – the pair of them, snapped in the MG as they were leaving the reception to go off on honeymoon.

He stared at himself from twenty years ago: thin face, unlined, thick curling hair. Now he had a double chin, was balding, wore a moustache and bifocals. Unrecognizable!

On the back of the MG was a 'Just married' placard, which obscured the middle two digits on the rear numberplate.

The girl must have gone to every photographer in the district until she found the one who had taken their wedding pictures. The negatives would have been on file, probably in a storeroom.

The girl had got a print. Then she had searched the *Evening Gazette*'s back issues for the paper's own picture of the same couple in the MG ... which would tell her the names and parents' addresses.

And there the search would stop, for Margaret's parents had emigrated long ago and his own parents were dead. He was safe.

Then it struck him like a blow. 'The electoral roll,' he said out loud. 'She simply goes through it, street by street, until she finds my name ...'

'Did you say something, Robert?' Margaret called.

'What? No, nothing.'

It would be only a matter of time now before his skeleton was out of its cupboard. He would be branded a child-killer, all the more heinous because he had covered his tracks (he had sold the MG immediately they had got back from honeymoon).

He would get at least five years for manslaughter. He would lose his job; his reputation would be ruined; everything he had built up over the years ... down the drain!

He knew he had not got the strength of character to begin all over again; he was too set in his ways . . .

'I think I'll got to The Swan for a pint, love. Don't wait up. I might be late.'

'Oh, all right. I'll leave something out for your supper.'

At times like this, he mused, it was positively an advantage having a conventionally predictable spouse.

It was a fifteen-minute drive to the block of service flats where the girl was staying; hers was on the ground floor.

She came to the door in a dressing-gown with a towel wrapped round her hair.

He was sorry to barge in on her unannounced, he blurted; but he had found himself in the neighbourhood, so he had thought he would give her that information about his friend.

'Oh, well, come in. You'll have to forgive my appearance – I'm in the middle of washing my hair. Can I get you a drink?'

'I won't, thanks – I'm driving.'

'Ah yes . . . the old breathalyser!'

He tried to smile but couldn't move his face muscles. 'That friend,' he began, swallowing. 'His name's . . . Smythe . . . Robert Smythe.'

'That's it,' she cried. 'The same one I've been looking for! I found his address this afternoon, in the electoral roll at the Town Hall.'

So it was true, he thought; she *was* tracking him down.

'Perhaps I will have that drink,' he said, slipping a hand into his jacket pocket.

She was at the drinks cabinet, her back to him. 'Gin and tonic all right?'

'Fine.' He pulled out a length of cord. It went round her neck so easily. He did not make a sound as he pulled it tight. Nor did she . . .

*

At the breakfast table next morning Margaret thought Robert looked pale and drawn; there were dark rings round his eyes and he seemed unusually preoccupied. Clearly he needed a holiday; he was working far too hard at that office.

She knew it probably would not be much good urging him to take the day off but she decided to try; to her surprise, he agreed.

'I do have a bit of a migraine, love,' he said.

'The rest will do you good. I'll ring the office and tell them you're not well.'

The 'plop' on the mat inside the front door told her the post had arrived. 'I'll go,' she said.

Two letters. One was Robert's bank statement, the other was for her. An unfamiliar handwriting.

She tore it open on her way back to the kitchen. It was a three-page letter, with a snapshot. The sudden shock, as she began to read, made her giddy.

. . . all I had to go on was your maiden name . . . you'd be surprised how many Margarets with that surname have got married since I was born . . . it meant checking each one to find if it was the right Margaret . . .

She stared at the attractive, fair-haired girl in the snap. Could it be . . . after all these years? It was something she had buried in her memory, something she had thought would remain buried; but, deep down, hadn't she always known she would never be able to escape from her past?

. . . when I first learned the truth about myself, I was hurt and angry . . . but now that I'm grown up myself, I'm able to understand why you did what you did . . .

She sat at the table and rested her hands on the scrubbed pine to stop them from trembling. She glanced at Robert but he seemed unaware of her agitation.

... finally traced you through your marriage to Robert Smythe ...
and now I feel I must meet you ... of course, my adoptive parents
will always be 'Mum' and 'Dad' to me but ...

Blinking back the tears, she heard Robert asking if the letter
was bad news.

'Bad? Oh no ...' Quite the contrary, she thought. But how
would her husband take it?

The guilt she had borne all those years suddenly overwhelmed her and she pushed the snapshot across the table.

'Robert, I don't quite know how to ... there's something
I've got to tell you ... something that happened before I met
you ...'

Mr Know-All

W. Somerset Maugham

I was prepared to dislike Max Kelada even before I knew him. The war had just finished and the passenger traffic in the ocean-going liners was heavy. Accommodation was very hard to get and you had to put up with whatever the agents chose to offer you. You could not hope for a cabin to yourself and I was thankful to be given one in which there were only two berths. But when I was told the name of my companion my heart sank. It suggested closed port-holes and the night air rigidly excluded. It was bad enough to share a cabin for fourteen days with anyone (I was going from San Francisco to Yokohama), but I should have looked upon it with less dismay if my fellow-passenger's name had been Smith or Brown.

When I went on board I found Mr Kelada's luggage already below. I did not like the look of it; there were too many labels on the suitcases, and the wardrobe trunk was too big. He had unpacked his toilet things, and I observed that he was a patron of the excellent Monsieur Coty; for I saw on the washing-stand his scent, his hair-wash, and his brilliantine. Mr Kelada's brushes, ebony with his monogram in gold, would have been all the better for a scrub. I did not at all like Mr Kelada. I made my way into the smoking-room. I called for a pack of cards and began to play patience. I had scarcely started before a man came up to me and asked me if he was right in thinking my name was so-and-so.

'I am Mr Kelada,' he added, with a smile that showed a row of flashing teeth, and sat down.

'Oh, yes, we're sharing a cabin, I think.'

'Bit of luck, I call it. You never know who you're going to be put in with. I was jolly glad when I heard you were English. I'm all for us English sticking together when we're abroad, if you understand what I mean.'

I blinked.

'Are you English?' I asked, perhaps tactlessly.

'Rather. You don't think I look an American, do you? British to the backbone, that's what I am.'

To prove it, Mr Kelada took out of his pocket a passport and airily waved it under my nose.

King George has many strange subjects. Mr Kelada was short and of a sturdy build, clean-shaven and dark-skinned, with a fleshy, hooked nose and very large, lustrous and liquid eyes. His long black hair was sleek and curly. He spoke with a fluency in which there was nothing English and his gestures were exuberant. I felt pretty sure that a closer inspection of that British passport would have betrayed the fact that Mr Kelada was born under a bluer sky than is generally seen in England.

'What will you have?' he asked me.

I looked at him doubtfully. Prohibition was in force and to all appearances the ship was bone-dry. When I am not thirsty I do not know which I dislike more, ginger-ale or lemon squash. But Mr Kelada flashed an oriental smile at me.

'Whisky and soda or dry Martini, you have only to say the word.'

From each of his hip-pockets he fished a flask and laid them on the table before me. I chose the Martini, and calling the steward he ordered a tumbler of ice and a couple of glasses.

'A very good cocktail,' I said.

'Well, there are plenty more where that came from, and if you've got any friends on board, you tell them you've got a pal who's got all the liquor in the world.'

Mr Kelada was chatty. He talked of New York and of San Francisco. He discussed plays, pictures, and politics. He was patriotic. The Union Jack is an impressive piece of drapery, but when it is flourished by a gentleman from Alexandria or Beirut, I cannot but feel that it loses somewhat in dignity. Mr Kelada was familiar. I do not wish to put on airs, but I cannot help feeling that it is seemly in a total stranger to put mister before my name when he addresses me. Mr Kelada, doubtless to set me at my ease, used no such formality. I did not like Mr Kelada. I had put aside the cards when he sat down, but now, thinking that for this first occasion our conversation had lasted long enough, I went on with my game.

'The three on the four,' said Mr Kelada.

There is nothing more exasperating when you are playing patience than to be told where to put the card you have turned up before you have had a chance to look for yourself.

'It's coming out, it's coming out,' he cried. 'The ten on the knave.'

With rage and hatred in my heart I finished. Then he seized the pack.

'Do you like card tricks?'

'No, I hate card tricks,' I answered.

'Well, I'll just show you this one.'

He showed me three. Then I said I would go down to the dining-room and get my seat at table.

'Oh, that's all right,' he said. 'I've already taken a seat for you. I thought that as we were in the same state-room we might just as well sit at the same table.'

I did not like Mr Kelada.

I not only shared a cabin with him and ate three meals a day at the same table, but I could not walk round the deck without his joining me. It was impossible to snub him. It never occurred to him that he was not wanted. He was certain that you were as glad to see him as he was to see you. In your own house you might have kicked him downstairs and slammed the door in his face without the suspicion dawning on him that he was not a welcome visitor. He was a good mixer, and in three days knew everyone on board. He ran everything. He managed the sweeps, conducted the auctions, collected money for prizes at the sports, got up quoit and golf matches, organized the concert, and arranged the fancy-dress ball. He was everywhere and always. He was certainly the best-hated man in the ship. We called him Mr Know-All, even to his face. He took it as a compliment. But it was at meal times that he was most intolerable. For the better part of an hour then he had us at his mercy. He was hearty, jovial, loquacious and argumentative. He knew everything better than anybody else, and it was an affront to his overweening vanity that you should disagree with him. He would not drop a subject, however unimportant, till he had brought you round to his way of thinking. The possibility that he could be mistaken never occurred to him. He was the chap who knew. We sat at the doctor's table. Mr Kelada would certainly have had it all his own way, for the doctor was lazy and I was frigidly indifferent, except for a man called Ramsay who sat there also. He was as dogmatic as Mr Kelada and resented bitterly the Levantine's cocksureness. The discussions they had were acrimonious and interminable.

Ramsay was in the American Consular Service, and was stationed at Kobe. He was a great heavy fellow from the Middle West, with loose fat under a tight skin, and he bulged out of his ready-made clothes. He was on his way back to resume his post, having been on a flying visit to New York to fetch his wife, who had been spending a year at home. Mrs Ramsay was a very pretty little thing, with pleasant manners and a sense of humour. The Consular Service is ill paid, and she was dressed always very simply; but she knew how to wear her clothes. She achieved an effect of quiet distinction. I should not have paid any particular attention to her but that she possessed a quality that may be common enough in women, but nowadays is not obvious in their demeanour. You could not look at her without being struck by her modesty. It shone in her like a flower on a coat.

One evening at dinner the conversation by chance drifted to the subject of pearls. There had been in the papers a good deal of talk about the culture pearls which the cunning Japanese were making, and the doctor remarked that they must inevitably diminish the value of the real ones. They were very good already; they would soon be perfect. Mr Kelada, as was his habit, rushed the new topic. He told us all that was to be known about pearls. I do not believe Ramsay knew anything about them at all, but he could not resist the opportunity to have a fling at the Levantine, and in five minutes we were in the middle of a heated argument. I had seen Mr Kelada vehement and voluble before, but never so voluble and vehement as now. At last something that Ramsay said stung him, for he thumped the table and shouted:

'Well, I ought to know what I am talking about. I'm going to Japan just to look into this Japanese pearl business. I'm in the trade and there's not a man in it who won't tell you that what I say about pearls goes. I know all the best pearls in the world, and what I don't know about pearls isn't worth knowing.'

Here was news for us, for Mr Kelada, with all his loquacity, had never told anyone what his business was. We only knew vaguely that he was going to Japan on some commercial errand. He looked round the table triumphantly.

'They'll never be able to get a culture pearl that an expert like me can't tell with half an eye.' He pointed to a chain that Mrs Ramsay wore. 'You take my word for it, Mrs Ramsay, that chain you're wearing will never be worth a cent less than it is now.'

Mrs Ramsay in her modest way flushed a little and slipped the chain inside her dress. Ramsay leaned forward. He gave us all a look and a smile flickered in his eyes.

'That's a pretty chain of Mrs Ramsay's, isn't it?'

'I noticed it at once,' answered Mr Kelada. 'Gee, I said to myself, those are pearls all right.'

'I didn't buy it myself, of course. I'd be interested to know how much you think it cost.'

'Oh, in the trade somewhere round fifteen thousand dollars. But if it was bought on Fifth Avenue I shouldn't be surprised to hear that anything up to thirty thousand was paid for it.'

Ramsay smiled grimly.

'You'll be surprised to hear that Mrs Ramsay bought that string at a department store the day before we left New York, for eighteen dollars.'

Mr Kelada flushed.

'Rot. It's not only real, but it's as fine a string for its size as I've ever seen.'

'Will you bet on it? I'll bet you a hundred dollars it's imitation.'

'Done.'

'Oh, Elmer, you can't bet on a certainty,' said Mrs Ramsay.

She had a little smile on her lips and her tone was gently deprecating.

'Can't I? If I get a chance of easy money like that I should be all sorts of a fool not to take it.'

'But how can it be proved?' she continued. 'It's only my word against Mr Kelada's.'

'Let me look at the chain, and if it's imitation I'll tell you quickly enough. I can afford to lose a hundred dollars,' said Mr Kelada.

'Take it off, dear. Let the gentleman look at it as much as he wants.'

Mrs Ramsay hesitated a moment. She put her hands to the clasp.

'I can't undo it,' she said. 'Mr Kelada will just have to take my word for it.'

I had a sudden suspicion that something unfortunate was about to occur, but I could think of nothing to say.

Ramsay jumped up.

'I'll do it.'

He handed the chain to Mr Kelada. The Levantine took a magnifying glass from his pocket and closely examined it. A smile of triumph spread over his smooth and swarthy face. He handed back the chain. He was about to speak. Suddenly he caught sight of Mrs Ramsay's face. It was so white that she looked as though she were about to faint. She was staring at him with wide and terrified eyes. They held a desperate appeal; it was so clear that I wondered why her husband did not see it.

Mr Kelada stopped with his mouth open. He flushed deeply. You could almost *see* the effort he was making over himself.

'I was mistaken,' he said. 'It's a very good imitation, but of course as soon as I looked through my glass I saw that it wasn't real. I think eighteen dollars is just about as much as the damned thing's worth.'

He took out his pocket-book and from it a hundred-dollar note. He handed it to Ramsay without a word.

'Perhaps that'll teach you not to be so cocksure another time, my young friend,' said Ramsay as he took the note.

I noticed that Mr Kelada's hands were trembling.

The story spread over the ship as stories do, and he had to put up with a good deal of chaff that evening. It was a fine joke that Mr Know-All had been caught out. But Mrs Ramsay retired to her state-room with a headache.

Next morning I got up and began to shave. Mr Kelada lay on his bed smoking a cigarette. Suddenly there was a small scraping sound and I saw a letter pushed under the door. I opened the door and looked out. There was nobody there. I picked up the letter and saw that it was addressed to Max Kelada. The name was written in block letters. I handed it to him.

'Who's this from?' He opened it. 'Oh!'

He took out of the envelope, not a letter, but a hundred-dollar note. He looked at me and again he reddened. He tore the envelope into little bits and gave them to me.

'Do you mind just throwing them out of the port-hole?'

I did as he asked, and then I looked at him with a smile.

'No one likes being made to look a perfect damned fool,' he said.

'Were the pearls real?'

'If I had a pretty little wife I shouldn't let her spend a year in New York while I stayed at Kobe,' said he.

At that moment I did not entirely dislike Mr Kelada. He reached out for his pocket-book and carefully put in it the hundred-dollar note.

The Colonel's Lady

W. Somerset Maugham

All this happened two or three years before the outbreak of the war.

The Peregrines were having breakfast. Though they were alone and the table was long they sat at opposite ends of it. From the walls George Peregrine's ancestors, painted by the fashionable painters of the day, looked down upon them. The butler brought in the morning post. There were several letters for the colonel, business letters, *The Times*, and a small parcel for his wife Evie. He looked at his letters and then, opening *The Times*, began to read it. They finished breakfast and rose from the table. He noticed that his wife hadn't opened the parcel.

'What's that?' he asked.

'Only some books.'

'Shall I open it for you?'

'If you like.'

He hated to cut string and so with some difficulty untied the knots.

'But they're all the same,' he said when he had unwrapped the parcel. 'What on earth d'you want six copies of the same book for?' He opened one of them. 'Poetry.' Then he looked at the title page. *When Pyramids Decay*, he read, by E. K. Hamilton. Eva Katherine Hamilton: that was his wife's maiden name. He looked at her with smiling surprise. 'Have you written a book, Evie? You are a slyboots.'

'I didn't think it would interest you very much. Would you like a copy?'

'Well, you know poetry isn't much in my line, but – yes, I'd like a copy; I'll read it. I'll take it along to my study. I've got a lot to do this morning.'

He gathered up *The Times*, his letters, and the book, and went out. His study was a large and comfortable room, with a big desk, leather arm-chairs, and what he called 'trophies of the chase' on the walls. On the bookshelves were works of reference, books on farming, gardening, fishing, and shooting, and books on the last war, in which he had won an MC and a DSO. For before his marriage he had been in the Welsh Guards. At the end of the war he retired and settled down to the life of a country gentleman in the spacious house, some twenty miles from Sheffield, which one of his forebears had built in the reign of George III. George Peregrine had an estate of some fifteen hundred acres which he managed with ability; he was a Justice of the Peace and performed his duties conscientiously. During the season he rode to hounds two days a week. He was a good shot, a golfer, and though now a little over fifty could still play a hard game of tennis. He could describe himself with propriety as an all-round sportsman.

He had been putting on weight lately, but was still a fine figure of a man; tall, with grey curly hair, only just beginning to grow thin on the crown, frank blue eyes, good features, and a high colour. He was a public-spirited man, chairman of any number of local organizations and, as became his class and station, a loyal member of the Conservative Party. He looked upon it as his duty to see to the welfare of the people on his estate and it was a satisfaction to him to know that Evie could be trusted to tend the sick and succour the poor. He had built a cottage hospital on the outskirts of the village and paid the wages of a nurse out of his own pocket. All he asked of the recipients of his bounty was that at elections, county or general, they should vote for his candidate. He was a friendly man, affable to his inferiors, considerate with his tenants, and popular with the neighbouring gentry. He would have been pleased and at the same time slightly embarrassed if someone had told him he was a jolly good fellow. That was what he wanted to be. He desired no higher praise.

It was hard luck that he had no children. He would have been an excellent father, kindly but strict, and would have brought up his sons as gentlemen's sons should be brought up, sent them to Eton, you know, taught them to fish, shoot, and ride. As it was, his heir was a nephew, son of his brother killed in a motor accident, not a bad boy, but not a chip off the old block, no, sir, far from it; and would you believe it, his fool of a mother was sending him to a co-educational school. Evie had been a sad disappointment to him. Of course she was a lady, and she had a bit of money of her own; she managed the house uncommonly well and she was a good hostess. The village people adored her. She had been a pretty little thing when he married her, with a creamy skin, light brown hair, and a trim figure, healthy too, and not a bad tennis player; he couldn't understand why she'd had no children; of course she was faded now, she must be getting on for five and forty; her skin was drab, her hair had lost its sheen, and she was as thin as a rail. She was always neat and suitably dressed, but she didn't seem to bother how she looked, she wore no make-up and didn't even use lipstick; sometimes at night when she dolled herself up for a party you could tell that once she'd been quite attractive, but ordinarily she was – well, the sort of woman you simply didn't notice. A nice woman, of course, a good wife, and it wasn't her fault if she was barren, but it was tough on a fellow who wanted an heir of his own loins; she hadn't any vitality, that's what was the matter with her. He supposed he'd been in love with her when he asked her to marry him, at least sufficiently in love for a man who wanted to marry and settle down, but with time he discovered that they had nothing much in common. She didn't care about hunting, and fishing bored her. Naturally they'd drifted apart. He had to do her the justice to admit that she'd never bothered him. There'd been no scenes. They had no quarrels. She seemed to take it for granted that he should go his own way. When he went up to London now and then she never wanted to come with him. He had a girl there, well, she wasn't exactly a girl, she was thirty-five if she was a day, but she was blonde and luscious and he only had to wire ahead of time and they'd dine, do a show, and spend the night together. Well, a man, a healthy normal man had to have some fun in his life. The thought crossed his mind that if Evie hadn't been such a good woman she'd have been a better wife; but it was not the sort of thought that he welcomed and he put it away from him.

George Peregrine finished his *Times* and being a considerate fellow rang the bell and told the butler to take it to Evie. Then he looked at his watch. It was half past ten and at eleven he had an appointment with one of his tenants. He had half an hour to spare.

'I'd better have a look at Evie's book,' he said to himself.

He took it up with a smile. Evie had a lot of highbrow books in her sitting-room, not the sort of books that interested him, but if they amused her he had no objection to her reading them. He noticed that the volume he now held in his hand contained no more than ninety pages. That was all to the good. He shared Edgar Allan Poe's opinion that poems should be short. But as he turned the pages he noticed that several of Evie's had long lines of irregular length and didn't rhyme. He didn't like that. At his first school, when he was a little boy, he remembered learning a poem that began: *The boy stood on the burning deck*, and later, at Eton, one that started: *Ruin seize thee, ruthless king*; and then there was *Henry V*; they'd had to take that, one half. He stared at Evie's pages with consternation.

'That's not what I call poetry,' he said.

Fortunately it wasn't all like that. Interspersed with the pieces that looked so odd, lines of three or four words and then a line of ten or fifteen, there were little poems, quite short, that rhymed, thank God, with the lines all the same length. Several of the pages were just headed with the word *Sonnet*, and out of curiosity he counted the lines; there were fourteen of them. He read them. They seemed all right, but he didn't quite know what they were all about. He repeated to himself: *Ruin seize thee, ruthless king.*

'Poor Evie,' he sighed.

At that moment the farmer he was expecting was ushered into the study, and putting the book down he made him welcome. They embarked on their business.

'I read your book, Evie,' he said as they sat down to lunch. 'Jolly good. Did it cost you a packet to have it printed?'

'No, I was lucky. I sent it to a publisher and he took it.'

'Not much money in poetry, my dear,' he said in his good-natured, hearty way.

'No, I don't suppose there is. What did Bannock want to see you about this morning?'

Bannock was the tenant who had interrupted his reading of Evie's poems.

'He's asked me to advance the money for a pedigree bull he wants to buy. He's a good man and I've half a mind to do it.'

George Peregrine saw that Evie didn't want to talk about her book and he was not sorry to change the subject. He was glad she had used her maiden name on the title page; he didn't suppose anyone would ever hear about the book, but he was proud of his own unusual name and he wouldn't have liked it if some damned penny-a-liner had made fun of Evie's effort in one of the papers.

During the few weeks that followed he thought it tactful not to ask Evie any questions about her venture into verse, and she never referred to it. It might have been a discreditable incident that they had silently agreed not to mention. But then a strange thing happened. He had to go to London on business and he took Daphne out to dinner. That was the name of the girl with whom he was in the habit of passing a few agreeable hours whenever he went to town.

'Oh, George,' she said, 'is that your wife who's written a book they're all talking about?'

'What on earth d'you mean?'

'Well, there's a fellow I know who's a critic. He took me out to dinner the other night and he had a book with him. "Got anything for me to read?" I said. "What's that?" "Oh, I don't think that's your cup of tea," he said. "It's poetry. I've just been reviewing it." "No poetry for me," I said. "It's about the hottest stuff I ever read," he said. "Selling like hot cakes. And it's damned good."'

'Who's the book by?' asked George.

'A woman called Hamilton. My friend told me that wasn't her real name. He said her real name was Peregrine. "Funny," I said, "I know a fellow called Peregrine." "Colonel in the army," he said. "Lives near Sheffield."'

'I'd just as soon you didn't talk about me to your friends,' said George with a frown of vexation.

'Keep your shirt on, dearie. Who d'you take me for? I just said: "It's not the same one."' Daphne giggled. 'My friend said: "They say he's a regular Colonel Blimp."'

George had a keen sense of humour.

'You could tell them better than that,' he laughed. 'If my wife had written a book I'd be the first to know about it, wouldn't I?'

'I suppose you would.'

Anyhow the matter didn't interest her and when the colonel began to talk of other things she forgot about it. He put it out of his mind too. There was nothing to it, he decided, and that silly fool of a critic had just been pulling Daphne's leg. He was amused at the thought of her tackling that book because she had been told it was hot stuff and then finding it just a lot of bosh cut up into unequal lines.

He was a member of several clubs and next day he thought

he'd lunch at one in St James's Street. He was catching a train back to Sheffield early in the afternoon. He was sitting in a comfortable arm-chair having a glass of sherry before going into the dining-room when an old friend came up to him.

'Well, old boy, how's life?' he said. 'How d'you like being the husband of a celebrity?'

George Peregrine looked at his friend. He thought he saw an amused twinkle in his eyes.

'I don't know what you're talking about,' he answered.

'Come off it, George. Everyone knows E. K. Hamilton is your wife. Not often a book of verse has a success like that. Look here, Henry Dashwood is lunching with me. He'd like to meet you.'

'Who the devil is Henry Dashwood and why should he want to meet me?'

'Oh, my dear fellow, what do you do with yourself all the time in the country? Henry's about the best critic we've got. He wrote a wonderful review of Evie's book. D'you mean to say she didn't show it you?'

Before George could answer his friend had called a man over. A tall, thin man, with a high forehead, a beard, a long nose, and a stoop, just the sort of man whom George was prepared to dislike at first sight. Introductions were effected. Henry Dashwood sat down.

'Is Mrs Peregrine in London by any chance? I should very much like to meet her,' he said.

'No, my wife doesn't like London. She prefers the country,' said George stiffly.

'She wrote me a very nice letter about my review. I was pleased. You know, we critics get more kicks than halfpence. I was simply bowled over by her book. It's so fresh and original, very modern without being obscure. She seems to be as much at her ease in free verse as in the classical metres.' Then because he was a critic he thought he should criticize. 'Sometimes her ear is a trifle at fault, but you can say the same of Emily

Dickinson. There are several of those short lyrics of hers that might have been written by Landor.'

All this was gibberish to George Peregrine. The man was nothing but a disgusting highbrow. But the colonel had good manners and he answered with proper civility; Henry Dashwood went on as though he hadn't spoken.

'But what makes the book so outstanding is the passion that throbs in every line. So many of these young poets are so anaemic, cold, bloodless, dully intellectual, but here you have real naked, earthy passion; of course deep, sincere emotion like that is tragic – ah, my dear Colonel, how right Heine was when he said that the poet makes little songs out of his great sorrows. You know, now and then, as I read and re-read those heart-rending pages I thought of Sappho.'

This was too much for George Peregrine and he got up.

'Well, it's jolly nice of you to say such nice things about my wife's little book. I'm sure she'll be delighted. But I must bolt, I've got to catch a train and I want to get a bite of lunch.'

'Damned fool,' he said irritably to himself as he walked upstairs to the dining-room.

He got home in time for dinner and after Evie had gone to bed he went into his study and looked for her book. He thought he'd just glance through it again to see for himself what they were making such a fuss about, but he couldn't find it. Evie must have taken it away.

'Silly,' he muttered.

He'd told her he thought it jolly good. What more could a fellow be expected to say? Well, it didn't matter. He lit his pipe and read the *Field* till he felt sleepy. But a week or so later it happened that he had to go into Sheffield for the day. He lunched there at his club. He had nearly finished when the Duke of Haverel came in. This was the great local magnate and of course the colonel knew him, but only to say how d'you do to; and he was surprised when the Duke stopped at his table.

'We're so sorry your wife wouldn't come to us for the weekend,' he said, with a sort of shy cordiality. 'We're expecting rather a nice lot of people.'

George was taken aback. He guessed that the Haverels had asked him and Evie over for the week-end and Evie, without saying a word to him about it, had refused. He had the presence of mind to say he was sorry too.

'Better luck next time,' said the Duke pleasantly and moved on.

Colonel Peregrine was very angry and when he got home he said to his wife:

'Look here, what's this about our being asked over to Haverel? Why on earth did you say we couldn't go? We've never been asked before and it's the best shooting in the county.'

'I didn't think of that. I thought it would only bore you.'

'Damn it all, you might at least have asked me if I wanted to go.'

'I'm sorry.'

He looked at her closely. There was something in her expression that he didn't quite understand. He frowned.

'I suppose *I* was asked?' he barked.

Evie flushed a little.

'Well, in point of fact you weren't.'

'I call it damned rude of them to ask you without asking me.'

'I suppose they thought it wasn't your sort of party. The Duchess is rather fond of writers and people like that, you know. She's having Henry Dashwood, the critic, and for some reason he wants to meet me.'

'It was damned nice of you to refuse, Evie.'

'It's the least I could do,' she smiled. She hesitated a moment. 'George, my publishers want to give a little dinner party for me one day towards the end of the month and of course they want you to come too.'

'Oh, I don't think that's quite my mark. I'll come up to London with you if you like. I'll find someone to dine with.'

Daphne.

'I expect it'll be very dull, but they're making rather a point of it. And the day after, the American publisher who's taken my book is giving a cocktail party at Claridge's. I'd like you to come to that if you wouldn't mind.'

'Sounds like a crashing bore, but if you really want me to come I'll come.'

'It would be sweet of you.'

George Peregrine was dazed by the cocktail party. There were a lot of people. Some of them didn't look so bad, a few of the women were decently turned out, but the men seemed to him pretty awful. He was introduced to everyone as Colonel Peregrine, E. K. Hamilton's husband, you know. The men didn't seem to have anything to say to him, but the women gushed.

'You *must* be proud of your wife. Isn't it *wonderful*? You know, I read it right through at a sitting, I simply couldn't put it down, and when I'd finished I started again at the beginning and read it right through a second time. I was simply *thrilled*.'

The English publisher said to him:

'We've not had a success like this with a book of verse for twenty years. I've never seen such reviews.'

The American publisher said to him:

'It's swell. It'll be a smash hit in America. You wait and see.'

The American publisher had sent Evie a great spray of orchids. Damned ridiculous, thought George. As they came in, people were taken up to Evie, and it was evident that they said flattering things to her, which she took with a pleasant smile and a word or two of thanks. She was a trifle flushed with the excitement, but seemed quite at her ease. Though he thought the whole thing a lot of stuff and nonsense George noted with approval that his wife was carrying it off in just the right way.

'Well, there's one thing,' he said to himself, 'you can see she's a lady and that's a damned sight more than you can say of anyone else here.'

He drank a good many cocktails. But there was one thing that bothered him. He had a notion that some of the people he was introduced to looked at him in rather a funny sort of way, he couldn't quite make out what it meant, and once when he strolled by two women who were sitting together on a sofa he had the impression that they were talking about him and after he passed he was almost certain they tittered. He was very glad when the party came to an end.

In the taxi on their way back to their hotel Evie said to him:

'You were wonderful, dear. You made quite a hit. The girls simply raved about you: they thought you so handsome.'

'Girls,' he said bitterly. 'Old hags.'

'Were you bored, dear?'

'Stiff.'

She pressed his hand in a gesture of sympathy.

'I hope you won't mind if we wait and go down by the afternoon train. I've got some things to do in the morning.'

'No, that's all right. Shopping?'

'I do want to buy one or two things, but I've got to go and be photographed. I hate the idea, but they think I ought to be. For America, you know.'

He said nothing. But he thought. He thought it would be a shock to the American public when they saw the portrait of the homely, desiccated little woman who was his wife. He'd always been under the impression that they liked glamour in America.

He went on thinking, and next morning when Evie had gone out he went to his club and up to the library. There he looked up recent numbers of *The Times Literary Supplement*, the *New Statesman*, and the *Spectator*. Presently he found reviews of Evie's book. He didn't read them very carefully, but enough to see that they were extremely favourable. Then he went to the bookseller's in Piccadilly where he occasionally bought books. He'd made up his mind that he had to read this damned thing of Evie's properly, but he didn't want to ask her what she'd done with the copy she'd given him. He'd buy one for himself. Before going in he looked in the window and the first thing he saw was a display of *When Pyramids Decay*. Damned silly title! He went in. A young man came forward and asked if he could help him.

'No, I'm just having a look round.' It embarrassed him to ask for Evie's book and he thought he'd find it for himself and then take it to the salesman. But he couldn't see it anywhere and at last, finding the young man near him, he said in a carefully casual tone: 'By the way, have you got a book called *When Pyramids Decay*?'

'The new edition came in this morning. I'll get a copy.'

In a moment the young man returned with it. He was a short, rather stout young man, with a shock of untidy carroty hair and spectacles. George Peregrine, tall, upstanding, very military, towered over him.

'Is this a new edition then?' he asked.

'Yes, sir. The fifth. It might be a novel the way it's selling.'

George Peregrine hesitated a moment.

'Why d'you suppose it's such a success? I've always been told no one reads poetry.'

'Well, it's good, you know. I've read it meself.' The young man, though obviously cultured, had a slight Cockney accent, and George quite instinctively adopted a patronizing attitude. 'It's the story they like. Sexy, you know, but tragic.'

George frowned a little. He was coming to the conclusion that the young man was rather impertinent. No one had told him anything about there being a story in the damned book and he had not gathered that from reading the reviews. The young man went on:

'Of course it's only a flash in the pan, if you know what I mean. The way I look at it, she was sort of inspired like by a personal experience, like Housman was with *The Shropshire Lad*. She'll never write anything else.'

'How much is the book?' said George coldly to stop his

chatter. 'You needn't wrap it up, I'll just slip it into my pocket.'

The November morning was raw and he was wearing a greatcoat.

At the station he bought the evening papers and magazines and he and Evie settled themselves comfortably in opposite corners of a first-class carriage and read. At five o'clock they went along to the restaurant car to have tea and chatted a little. They arrived. They drove home in the car which was waiting for them. They bathed, dressed for dinner, and after dinner Evie, saying she was tired out, went to bed. She kissed him, as was her habit, on the forehead. Then he went into the hall, took Evie's book out of his greatcoat pocket and going into the study began to read it. He didn't read verse very easily and though he read with attention, every word of it, the impression he received was far from clear. Then he began at the beginning again and read it a second time. He read with increasing malaise, but he was not a stupid man and when he had finished he had a distinct understanding of what it was all about. Part of the book was in free verse, part in conventional metres, but the story it related was coherent and plain to the meanest intelligence. It was the story of a passionate love affair between an older woman, married, and a young man. George Peregrine made out the steps of it as easily as if he had been doing a sum in simple addition.

Written in the first person, it began with the tremulous surprise of the woman, past her youth, when it dawned upon her that the young man was in love with her. She hesitated to believe it. She thought she must be deceiving herself. And she was terrified when on a sudden she discovered that she was passionately in love with him. She told herself it was absurd; with the disparity of age between them nothing but unhappiness could come to her if she yielded to her emotion. She tried to prevent him from speaking but the day came when he told her that he loved her and forced her to tell him that she loved him too. He begged her to run away with him. She couldn't leave her husband, her home; and what life could they look forward to, she an ageing woman, he so young? How could she expect his love to last? She begged him to have mercy on her. But his love was impetuous. He wanted her, he wanted her with all his heart, and at last trembling, afraid, desirous, she yielded to him. Then there was a period of ecstatic happiness. The world, the dull, humdrum world of every day, blazed with glory. Love songs flowed from her pen. The woman worshipped the young, virile body of her lover. George flushed darkly when she praised his broad chest and slim flanks, the beauty of his legs and the flatness of his belly.

Hot stuff, Daphne's friend had said. It was that all right. Disgusting.

There were sad little pieces in which she lamented the emptiness of her life when as must happen he left her, but they ended with a cry that all she had to suffer would be worth it for the bliss that for a while had been hers. She wrote of the long, tremulous nights they passed together and the languor that lulled them to sleep in one another's arms. She wrote of the rapture of brief stolen moments when, braving all danger, their passion overwhelmed them and they surrendered to its call.

She thought it would be an affair of a few weeks, but miraculously it lasted. One of the poems referred to three years having gone by without lessening the love that filled their hearts. It looked as though he continued to press her to go away with him, far away, to a hill town in Italy, a Greek island, a walled city in Tunisia, so that they could be together always, for in another of the poems she besought him to let things be as they were. Their happiness was precarious. Perhaps it was owing to the difficulties they had to encounter and the rarity of their meetings that their love had retained for so long its first enchanting ardour. Then on a sudden the young man died. How, when or where George could not discover. There followed a long, heartbroken cry of bitter grief, grief she could not indulge in, grief that had to be hidden. She had to be cheerful, give dinner-parties and go out to dinner, behave as she had always behaved, though the light had gone out of her life and she was bowed down with anguish. The last poem of all was a set of four short stanzas in which the writer, sadly resigned to her loss, thanked the dark powers that rule man's destiny that she had been privileged at least for a while to enjoy the greatest happiness that we poor human beings can ever hope to know.

It was three o'clock in the morning when George Peregrine finally put the book down. It had seemed to him that he heard Evie's voice in every line, over and over again he came upon turns of phrase he had heard her use, there were details that were as familiar to him as to her: there was no doubt about it; it was her own story she had told, and it was as plain as anything could be that she had had a lover and her lover had died. It was not anger so much that he felt, nor horror or dismay, though he was dismayed and he was horrified, but amazement. It was as inconceivable that Evie should have had a love affair, and a wildly passionate one at that, as that the trout in a glass case over the chimney piece in his study, the finest he had ever caught, should suddenly wag its tail. He understood now the meaning of the amused look he had seen in the eyes of that man he had spoken to at the club, he understood why Daphne when she was talking about the book had seemed to be enjoying a private joke, and why those two women at the cocktail party had tittered when he strolled past them.

He broke out into a sweat. Then on a sudden he was seized with fury and he jumped up to go and awake Evie and ask her sternly for an explanation. But he stopped at the door. After all, what proof had he? A book. He remembered that he'd told Evie he thought it jolly good. True, he hadn't read it, but he'd pretended he had. He would look a perfect fool if he had to admit that.

'I must watch my step,' he muttered.

He made up his mind to wait for two or three days and think it all over. Then he'd decide what to do. He went to bed, but he couldn't sleep for a long time.

'Evie,' he kept on saying to himself. 'Evie, of all people.'

They met at breakfast next morning as usual. Evie was as she always was, quiet, demure, and self-possessed, a middle-aged woman who made no effort to look younger than she was, a woman who had nothing of what he still called It. He looked at her as he hadn't looked at her for years. She had her usual placid serenity. Her pale blue eyes were untroubled. There was no sign of guilt on her candid brow. She made the same little casual remarks she always made.

'It's nice to get back to the country again after those two hectic days in London. What are you going to do this morning?'

It was incomprehensible.

Three days later he went to see his solicitor. Henry Blane was an old friend of George's as well as his lawyer. He had a place not far from Peregrine's and for years they had shot over one another's preserves. For two days a week he was a country gentleman and for the other five a busy lawyer in Sheffield. He was a tall, robust fellow, with a boisterous manner and a jovial laugh, which suggested that he liked to be looked upon essentially as a sportsman and a good fellow and only incidentally as a lawyer. But he was shrewd and worldy-wise.

'Well, George, what's brought you here today?' he boomed as the colonel was shown into his office. 'Have a good time in London? I'm taking my missus up for a few days next week. How's Evie?'

'It's about Evie I've come to see you,' said Peregrine, giving him a suspicious look. 'Have you read her book?'

His sensitivity had been sharpened during those last days of troubled thought and he was conscious of a faint change in the lawyer's expression. It was as though he were suddenly on his guard.

'Yes, I've read it. Great success, isn't it? Fancy Evie breaking out into poetry. Wonders will never cease.'

George Peregrine was inclined to lose his temper.

'It's made me look a perfect damned fool.'

'Oh, what nonsense, George! There's no harm in Evie's writing a book. You ought to be jolly proud of her.'

'Don't talk such rot. It's her own story. You know it and everyone else knows it. I suppose I'm the only one who doesn't know who her lover was.'

'There is such a thing as imagination, old boy. There's no reason to suppose the whole thing isn't made up.'

'Look here, Henry, we've known one another all our lives. We've had all sorts of good times together. Be honest with me. Can you look me in the face and tell me you believe it's a made-up story?'

Harry Blane moved uneasily in his chair. He was disturbed by the distress in old George's voice.

'You've got no right to ask me a question like that. Ask Evie.'

'I daren't,' George answered after an anguished pause. 'I'm afraid she'd tell me the truth.'

There was an uncomfortable silence.

'Who was the chap?'

Harry Blane looked at him straight in the eye.

'I don't know, and if I did I wouldn't tell you.'

'You swine. Don't you see what a position I'm in? Do you think it's very pleasant to be made absolutely ridiculous?'

The lawyer lit a cigarette and for some moments silently puffed it.

'I don't see what I can do for you,' he said at last.

'You've got private detectives you employ, I suppose. I want you to put them on the job and let them find everything out.'

'It's not very pretty to put detectives on one's wife, old boy; and besides, taking for granted for a moment that Evie had an affair, it was a good many years ago and I don't suppose it would be possible to find out a thing. They seem to have covered their tracks pretty carefully.'

'I don't care. You put the detectives on. I want to know the truth.'

'I won't, George. If you're determined to do that you'd better consult someone else. And look here, even if you got evidence that Evie had been unfaithful to you what would you do with it? You'd look rather silly divorcing your wife because she'd committed adultery ten years ago.'

'At all events I could have it out with her.'

'You can do that now, but you know just as well as I do that if you do she'll leave you. D'you want her to do that?'

George gave him an unhappy look.

'I don't know. I always thought she'd been a damned good wife to me. She runs the house perfectly, we never have any servant trouble; she's done wonders with the garden and she's splendid with all the village people. But damn it, I have my self-respect to think of. How can I go on living with her when I know that she was grossly unfaithful to me?'

'Have you always been faithful to her?'

'More or less, you know. After all, we've been married for nearly twenty-four years and Evie was never much for bed.'

The solicitor slightly raised his eyebrows, but George was too intent on what he was saying to notice.

'I don't deny that I've had a bit of fun now and then. A man wants it. Women are different.'

'We only have men's word for that,' said Harry Blane, with a faint smile.

'Evie's absolutely the last woman I'd have suspected of kicking over the traces. I mean, she's a very fastidious, reticent woman. What on earth made her write the damned book?'

'I suppose it was a very poignant experience and perhaps it was a relief to her to get it off her chest like that.'

'Well, if she had to write it why the devil didn't she write it under an assumed name?'

'She used her maiden name. I suppose she thought that was enough, and it would have been if the book hadn't had this amazing boom.'

George Peregrine and the lawyer were sitting opposite one another with a desk between them. George, his elbow on the desk, his cheek on his hand, frowned at his thought.

'It's so rotten not to know what sort of a chap he was. One can't even tell if he was by way of being a gentleman. I mean, for all I know he may have been a farm-hand or a clerk in a lawyer's office.'

Harry Blane did not permit himself to smile and when he answered there was in his eyes a kindly, tolerant look.

'Knowing Evie so well I think the probabilities are that he was all right. Anyhow I'm sure he wasn't a clerk in my office.'

'It's been a shock to me,' the colonel sighed. 'I thought she was fond of me. She couldn't have written that book unless she hated me.'

'Oh, I don't believe that. I don't think she's capable of hatred.'

'You're not going to pretend that she loves me.'

'No.'

'Well, what does she feel for me?'

Harry Blane leaned back in his swivel chair and looked at George reflectively.

'Indifference, I should say.'

The colonel gave a little shudder and reddened.

'After all, you're not in love with her, are you?'

George Peregrine did not answer directly.

'It's been a great blow to me not to have any children, but I've never let her see that I think she's let me down. I've always been kind to her. Within reasonable limits I've tried to do my duty by her.'

The lawyer passed a large hand over his mouth to conceal the smile that trembled on his lips.

'It's been such an awful shock to me,' Peregrine went on. 'Damn it all, even ten years ago Evie was no chicken and God knows, she wasn't much to look at. It's so ugly.' He sighed deeply. 'What would *you* do in my place?'

'Nothing.'

George Peregrine drew himself bolt upright in his chair and he looked at Harry with the stern set face that he must have worn when he inspected his regiment.

'I can't overlook a thing like this. I've been made a laughing-stock. I can never hold up my head again.'

'Nonsense,' said the lawyer sharply, and then in a pleasant, kindly manner, 'Listen, old boy: the man's dead; it all happened a long while back. Forget it. Talk to people about Evie's book, rave about it, tell 'em how proud you are of her. Behave as though you had so much confidence in her, you *knew* she could never have been unfaithful to you. The world moves so quickly and people's memories are so short. They'll forget.'

'I shan't forget.'

'You're both middle-aged people. She probably does a great deal more for you than you think and you'd be awfully lonely without her. I don't think it matters if you don't forget. It'll be all to the good if you can get it into that thick head of yours that there's a lot more in Evie than you ever had the gumption to see.'

'Damn it all, you talk as if I was to blame.'

'No, I don't think you were to blame, but I'm not so sure that Evie was either. I don't suppose she wanted to fall in love with this boy. D'you remember those verses right at the end? The impression they gave me was that though she was shattered by his death, in a strange way she welcomed it. All through she'd been aware of the fragility of the tie that bound them. He died in the full flush of his first love and had never known that love so seldom endures; he'd only known its bliss and beauty. In her own bitter grief she found solace in the thought that he'd been spared all sorrow.'

'All that's a bit above my head, old boy. I see more or less what you mean.'

George Peregrine stared unhappily at the inkstand on the desk. He was silent and the lawyer looked at him with curious, yet sympathetic, eyes.

'Do you realize what courage she must have had never by a sign to show how dreadfully unhappy she was?' he said gently.

Colonel Peregrine sighed.

'I'm broken. I suppose you're right; it's no good crying over spilt milk and it would only make things worse if I made a fuss.'

'Well?'

George Peregrine gave a pitiful little smile.

'I'll take your advice. I'll do nothing. Let them think me a damned fool and to hell with them. The truth is, I don't know what I'd do without Evie. But I'll tell you what, there's one thing I shall never understand till my dying day: What in the name of heaven did the fellow ever see in her?'

Wink Three Times

John Charters

Amanda Winterton was about to lose her virginity.

The thought coursed through her, deliciously, making her feel faint, her eyes closing and her breath coming quicker. She opened the drawer of her typing desk and pretended to search for a pencil in case the other girls in the office noticed her flushed face, made fun of her again in their senseless, cruel way; the 'old maid' they called her behind her back, sometimes in front of her as well.

Because they were young and pretty, wore tiny skirts and flaunted their legs at every salesman who came in, swore vividly and talked shockingly, was no reason, in Amanda's opinion, for them to treat her like a leper. She was only thirty-eight, a little too thin and a little too tall, admittedly, but with a long serious face and big dark eyes. She wore her hair in a bun because if she let it down it would swing into the typewriter.

For seventeen long years, since her mother died, she had looked after her crippled father. Left with only a small pension from an unfeeling society, which cared not whether he lived or died, he had clung to a grim life with the loving help of Amanda. Mainly confined to a wheelchair, he depended on her as his only living relative. They lived in the small apartment all these years, every day the same routine: preparing his breakfast, setting out his cold lunch, then dashing to the office; hurrying home at night to cook his dinner, then keeping him company, talking, sometimes watching the black-and-white television set, unable to afford a colour one, then to bed; and the whole process repeated the next day.

Occasionally on Saturday she would have a 'date' and go to the local cinema. But she was not beautiful and usually the friend would become bored with her excuse that she had to return to look after her father, who could not be left alone for long. Whether they believed her or not, it resulted in an abortive friendship, and she would wait many weeks before another man would find her sufficiently interesting to take out.

It had not depressed her, nor made her bitter. She loved her father and had come to realize that not everyone can live a happy life all the time; she had accepted her burden in life cheerfully, thankful she was alive and healthy, appreciating that she could jump on a bus or run up stairs, something her father would never do again. After several years she realized there was no chance of getting married; no man would take on the responsibility of a crippled father-in-law. She did not mind. One could live without sex and marriage if one shut one's eyes tightly and pretended it didn't exist, not even in the middle of a warm night when one awoke with treacherous body aflame and awful, pulsating desires.

Her work as the manager's secretary was interesting, the only flaw being that she shared her big office with four others, all young and attractive and sophisticated. They did not hate, nor even despise her. She was just the 'old maid', the boss's secretary, who one ignored unless there was nothing better to do and then it was fun to taunt her, or say a mild 'fuck' and watch her blush and pretend not to hear.

She looked up and saw Irene, a pert young red-head with long slim legs, watching her.

'Something wrong, Amanda? You look very flushed, dear. Is it the curse?'

Eileen, sleek and sophisticated and perpetually bored, looked up from her desk.

'Bit late for that, isn't it? I thought it stopped with the change-of-life.'

For once Amanda rode the conversation without shrinking.

'What a shame you girls have cess-pits for minds. Did you study very hard to achieve it? Or did you even go to school? Do you know Pythagoras's theorem?'

'No, but I've seen his cock!' All the girls burst into roaring laughter at Irene's clever reply. Even Amanda smiled, nothing could upset her today. She looked at her watch and saw it was almost five. Roll on, minutes, roll on towards my destiny, my defloration, that I may be taken and made whole, a real live woman.

Three months earlier her father had awakened in the middle of the night, shouting for her, complaining of pains in his head. She had thrown on a dressing-gown and rushed into his bedroom. Within minutes she had telephoned the doctor, who arrived half an hour later. By then he was dead. Haemorrhage of the brain, the doctor diagnosed.

For the next two months she lived in a void, unable to comprehend that for the first time in her life she was alone, that she need not rush back from the office, there was no necessity to cook dinner, to do all the shopping on Saturday morning. Now she could go out, see things, come in at mid-night or three in the morning if she wished. She was alone.

One day on the bus to work she had seen the advertisement in the Personal column:

Escort Service. Girls, do you need a handsome companion to take you out, dine with you, show off to your friends? Our male models are attentive and well-educated. Send for details to . . .

For days she had re-read it, wondering if she dare send in her name, or how to explain what she wanted: to be seduced. One night after drinking two glasses of sherry, suitably fortified, she wrote the letter:

Dear Sirs,

Referring to your advertisement, I shall be in town next
Friday evening and will require an escort. He need not be
too young or too handsome, as I myself am thirty-eight. I
shall require him to come to the Bilton Towers Hotel at nine
p.m., and ask for me at the desk. I enclose 30 dollars on
account.

Yours truly,
(Miss) Amanda Winterton

She was pleased with the letter, after re-drafting it several
times. It looked innocent and business-like. She considered using
an assumed name, but felt it would be too complicated and
unnecessary; after all, she was a perfectly legitimate lady asking
for an escort for the evening. After he arrived it would be
different.

A few days later the reply had arrived from the agency,
confirming the appointment and stating that Mr Charles
Hackforth would come to her hotel at nine o'clock on Friday
evening, wearing a dark suit unless a tuxedo was particularly
required; if so, the fee would be slightly higher. It ended primly
by reminding Miss Winterton that those employed by the
Escort Service were 'perfect gentlemen' and they were sure she
would be very satisfied.

I'll let you know that the next morning, thought Amanda.

She wondered how much money she should take with her.
Would he accept 100 dollars? She could have saved money by
bringing him up to her apartment, but the memory of her
father was still vivid, and somehow she felt an hotel suite would
be easier and more appropriate to the occasion.

She booked the suite at the Bilton Towers by telephone,
feeling delightfully guilty. Now it was Friday night and time to
leave the office. She looked up at the other girls fondly. Next
time she saw them on Monday morning she would be one of

them, no longer a leper, no longer a virgin. She wondered if they would notice.

Charlie Parker was in a fine mood as he drove into the city, although he frequently cursed as he found himself in the wrong line of traffic. How these townfolk could live in such a mass of steel and concrete and glass was beyond his imagination, but at least it kept them clear of his beautiful countryside.

It was a stroke of luck that the Old Man had given him the job of signing the Tel-Tractor contract. Normally this was Ben's territory, but at the last moment Ben had succumbed to a bout of flu, and the Old Man did not want to postpone such an important contract with a big client. So Charlie had been pulled off his usual route and told to get his ass up to the city. They had even booked him into the swank Bilton Towers Hotel, which was O K by him too; he'd never stayed in one of those ritzy places.

Charlie smiled at himself in the driving mirror, undismayed by the craggy face with the thinning hair that returned the smile. He had never cared about his looks, although over the past two years he had half-heartedly started to do exercises each morning to reduce his middle-aged paunch. It hadn't had much effect. He was a good salesman and loved his work, making many friends amongst his farmer clients. He ate well and drank well, and when he could he whored well. He had never married, believing that a good salesman should not be tied down by constantly thinking of home.

He pulled into the curb and asked a passer-by the way to the Bilton Towers. The man looked at him, sensing a country hick, bitingly told him to look across the road, are you fooling me, bud? Sure enough, the vast skyscraper had *The Bilton Towers* in a glittering neon sign across the entrance. His problem was that he had to cross eight lines of thundering traffic to get there. With a friendly thanks to his sarcastic informant he put out his indicator, stuck out a brown weather-beaten hand and gunned the Chev into the lanes of cars. In a moment there was a pandemonium of screeching brakes and hooting horns. Unperturbed, Charlie continued diagonally across the road, pulling up in front of the carpeted pavement to the delight and amusement of the splendidly uniformed negro commissionaire.

'Man, that was something. You sure must be from out of town, sir,' he chuckled, opening the door for Charlie. 'Leave the key, I'll take it. Your baggage will be sent up, sir. The name?'

'Parker. Charlie Parker. Thanks.' He slid a note into the black hand and strode into the lobby.

Amanda Winterton walked slowly round the sumptuous suite, appreciating the heavy quality of the furniture, the deep pile of the carpet, peering at the paintings on the wall and pieces of sculpture in lighted niches. In the bedroom, where her de-flowering would take place, she looked with anticipation and pleasure at the blue silk cover, the blue carpet and curtains, thinking how snug and comfortable it all looked. She hoped she would not have trouble getting Mr Charles Hackforth into bed; she could only go by instinct and the books she had read over the years.

Now came the tricky part of her plan. She sat down at the Sheraton-style writing desk and took a piece of the ornate hotel writing paper out of the drawer. She wrote in her neat handwriting:

Dear Mr Hackforth,

My plans have changed slightly, and I will not be here when you arrive. Please will you ask for the key to my suite, 2122, go up there and wait for me. I have left some whisky and ice, please help yourself. I should be back shortly.

Yours sincerely,
Amanda Winterton

She put it in a matching envelope, sealed it, and wrote *Charles Hackforth* in large letters. She turned out all the lights except a dim one over the sideboard, showing where the bottle of Scotch rested. She took the elevator to the lobby and gave the letter and the key to 2212 to the head porter; it was a few minutes to nine and she crossed over to the well-patronized buffet-bar to while away some time.

Charlie Parker had dined well on the company's expense account, and had lubricated himself liberally with dry martinis and a half bottle of wine. He thought with envy that this was the life, that lucky dog Ben had one helluva territory to cover, whereas he himself usually stayed in a small one-star hotel in a farming town where one ate at the local drug-store, hash or steak and French fries, a can of beer, and the eternal Aunt Mabel's famous apple-pie.

It was nearly nine o'clock, Charlie was pleasantly tired after the long drive, and his appointment with the Vice-President of Tel-Tractors was at ten a.m. the next day. ('An' you be there real sharp, boy,' the Old Man had admonished, ''cos he's comin' in on Saturday mornin' jest to sign this contract!') It would be a pleasure to crawl into his silken bed in the posh suite they had given him, all fancy like the President's House – it was almost sacrilege to use it. He stood up, signed the bill with a flourish, realizing he was just a *little* high, and carefully walked out of the big dining-room.

The lobby was crowded, he stood by the porter's desk while two harassed attendants handed over keys and wrote down special calls and instructions. Sleepily he watched the mass of people till the porter asked him suddenly:

'Yes, sir. What room number?'

'Huh? Oh, 2212 please.'

The porter scooped up the key and handed it to him. A fat woman pushed him aside and trod on his foot, giving him a glare for having it in the way. He apologized politely and sauntered to the elevators.

Somewhere up the huge skyscraper he was spewed out on to the thickly carpeted corridor. He commenced the long walk to his room, following a confusing sign-post of numbers. He wondered how many miles of carpet had been used, trying to work out the length of each corridor, the height of the building, and the number of floors. It came to a staggering figure; his mind boggled. He put the key in the lock and opened the door.

There was a single light burning, the maid must have been in, a cute little girl who had interrupted him earlier when he was taking a bath, apologizing prettily, saying she would come back later with clean towels. Charlie had been impressed; it seemed every time you washed your hands someone ran in with a clean towel.

There was a bottle of good Scotch on the sideboard, another impressive part of the hotel service. He wondered if they put a bottle in every room, or only these fancy suites. He poured himself a stiff one and drank it as he switched on the bedroom lights and started to undress. He couldn't find his pyjamas, but was too tired to care.

Amanda had sat demurely in a corner and slowly drunk two brandies, her excitement rising as the time passed. She wondered what it would be like. Would it be painful the first time? Would he be rough and cruel, or kind and understanding? She refused to allow herself to think he might not want her, might stiffly walk out of the room. Surely that was not possible, not an escort man; even if they were 'perfect gentlemen' they must occasionally have the odd flutter, especially when she was paying him; to him it would be part of the service, obeying instructions of the client; after all she wasn't fat and really ugly or old, only thirty-eight and she would let down her hair which made her look younger . . .

It was time to go. Her heart was beating rapidly as she paid the waiter, returning his curious stare to show she was not a pick-up. She walked across the lobby, noting it was after nine-thirty. Mr Hackforth should have collected her message and the key half an hour ago. She asked for 2212 and with relief heard the porter say it was already out. She apologized and crossed to the elevators.

She came down the long corridor and stopped outside her door, noting the key was in the lock. Good. Gently she opened the door, expecting to see him sitting there, welcoming her, the man who was to take her virginity. She was disappointed. The room was empty, the single light still on. But with satisfaction she noted the whisky had sunk several inches. Perhaps he was in the bathroom?

She crossed to the bedroom, saw to her surprise there was a man in her bed. She had an insane desire to giggle, it was like the *Three Bears*. Well! He was being presumptuous, but perhaps this was what always happened when they were asked up to the bedroom, perhaps her little ruse had unwittingly been an old ploy, and he had read her note and groaned and thought, 'One of those again'. He seemed to be sound asleep, too, which wasn't very flattering to her.

She debated waking him, decided to get undressed first so there would be no embarrassment later. She crossed quietly to the bathroom and closed the door. Quickly she undressed and slipped on the black diaphanous nightie she had bought for the occasion. She had showered and perfumed herself an hour earlier. She let down her long hair, giving it a few strokes with a brush, noting the effect in the long mirror. She saw a thin but not unattractive face, glowing black hair falling to the waist, a white slim body barely visible through the nightgown, huge brown eyes, now scared but determined. She switched off the light and came back into the bedroom.

Charlie Parker stirred and thought sleepily it was a helluva bed, soft and springy. He had been having a wonderful dream about a girl, he couldn't remember what it was about, but it sure was a mighty fine hotel. He would kid Ben about his luxury living.

Unbelievably, he felt the bedclothes being lifted and a body slipping into the bed, a body smelling deliciously of woman and perfume. He had left the small light on in the sitting-room, and as he turned round he could see a madonna-like face with large eyes on the pillow next to him. There must be a mistake, he thought wildly, she's going to scream any moment. A pair of soft arms came round his neck.

'I'm sorry I kept you waiting, Charles. I'm here now, I'm ready, dear Charles . . .'

The difference between 2122 and 2212 may not appear to be large, but it can alter many lives. Down the corridor on the same floor an impatient Mr Hackforth sat waiting in an armchair. He wondered why there was a pair of men's pyjamas laid out on the bed, deciding that with Women's Lib these days nothing was sacred.

Groggily, Charlie opened one eye, wincing at the strong sunlight pouring into the room. For a moment he remembered the impossible dream and the incredible night that followed. Abruptly he sat up; it had been no dream and he could still smell the lingering perfume. Most of the bedclothes were on the floor.

He looked at his watch. It was nine o'clock. In a panic in case he was late for the Vice-President of Tel-Tractors, he jumped out of the bed and started to dress. He would get a shave downstairs in the barber-shop while he had some coffee.

There was no sign of the girl, the incredible girl who had played the innocent virgin, played it damn well, too, because he had performed better than ever in his life, all through the night she demanded more, and incredibly, he had obliged. Jesus, he thought as he strode into the sitting-room, she was sensational; and so was I, he concluded modestly.

On the mantelpiece, next to the bottle of whisky was a piece of writing paper. Pinned to it was a hundred dollar note.

Dearest Charles,

Forgive me for leaving you before you awoke, but I am a working girl and must be in my office by nine.

You have given me a new life and a new meaning to my life. Don't be offended if I leave a little something for you. You were kind, sweet and wonderful.

Always I shall remember you.

A. W.

He shook his head disbelievingly as he walked along to the elevators. He wondered what his bill would be downstairs; whatever it was it was worth it, what incredible service, even to the broad knowing my name, he thought, and leaving that note to make me feel good.

'Hot damn!' he said aloud, 'these modern hotels are the greatest!'

The Verger

W. Somerset Maugham

There had been a christening that afternoon at St Peter's, Neville Square, and Albert Edward Foreman still wore his verger's gown. He kept his new one, its folds as full and stiff as though it were made not of alpaca but of perennial bronze, for funerals and weddings (St Peter's, Neville Square, was a church much favoured by the fashionable for these ceremonies) and now he wore only his second-best. He wore it with complacence, for it was the dignified symbol of his office, and without it (when he took it off to go home) he had the disconcerting sensation of being somewhat insufficiently clad. He took pains with it; he pressed it and ironed it himself. During the sixteen years he had been verger of this church he had had a succession of such gowns, but he had never been able to throw them away when they were worn out and the complete series, neatly wrapped up in brown paper, lay in the bottom drawers of the wardrobe in his bedroom.

The verger busied himself quietly, replacing the painted wooden cover on the marble font, taking away a chair that had been brought for an infirm old lady, and waited for the vicar to have finished in the vestry so that he could tidy up in there and go home. Presently he saw him walk across the chancel, genuflect in front of the high altar, and come down the aisle; but he still wore his cassock.

'What's he 'anging about for?' the verger said to himself. 'Don't 'e know I want my tea?'

The vicar had been but recently appointed, a red-faced energetic man in the early forties, and Albert Edward still regretted his predecessor, a clergyman of the old school who preached leisurely sermons in a silvery voice and dined out a great deal with his more aristocratic parishioners. He liked things in church to be just so, but he never fussed; he was not like this new man who wanted to have his finger in every pie. But Albert Edward was tolerant. St Peter's was in a very good neighbourhood and the parishioners were a very nice class of people. The new vicar had come from the East End and he couldn't be expected to fall in all at once with the discreet ways of his fashionable congregation.

'All this 'ustle,' said Albert Edward. 'But give 'im time, he'll learn.'

When the vicar had walked down the aisle so far that he could address the verger without raising his voice more than was becoming in a place of worship he stopped.

'Foreman, will you come into the vestry for a minute. I have something to say to you.'

'Very good, sir.'

The vicar waited for him to come up and they walked up the church together.

'A very nice christening, I thought, sir. Funny 'ow the baby stopped cryin' the moment you took him.'

'I've noticed they very often do,' said the vicar, with a little smile. 'After all I've had a good deal of practice with them.'

It was a source of subdued pride to him that he could nearly always quiet a whimpering infant by the manner in which he held it and he was not unconscious of the amused admiration with which mothers and nurses watched him settle the baby in the crook of his surpliced arm. The verger knew that it pleased him to be complimented on his talent.

The vicar preceded Albert Edward into the vestry. Albert Edward was a trifle surprised to find the two churchwardens there. He had not seen them come in. They gave him pleasant nods.

'Good afternoon, my lord. Good afternoon, sir,' he said to one after the other.

They were elderly men, both of them, and they had been churchwardens almost as long as Albert Edward had been verger. They were sitting now at a handsome refectory table that the old vicar had brought many years before from Italy and the vicar sat down in the vacant chair between them. Albert Edward faced them, the table between him and them, and wondered with slight uneasiness what was the matter. He remembered still the occasion on which the organist had got into trouble and the bother they had all had to hush things up. In a church like St Peter's, Neville Square, they couldn't afford a scandal. On the vicar's red face was a look of resolute benignity, but the others bore an expression that was slightly troubled.

'He's been naggin' them, he 'as,' said the verger to himself. 'He's jockeyed them into doin' something, but they don't 'alf like it. That's what it is, you mark my words.'

But his thoughts did not appear on Albert Edward's clean-cut and distinguished features. He stood in a respectful but not obsequious attitude. He had been in service before he was appointed to his ecclesiastical office, but only in very good houses, and his deportment was irreproachable. Starting as a page-boy in the household of a merchant-prince, he had risen by due degrees from the position of fourth to first footman, for a year he had been single-handed butler to a widowed peeress, and, till the vacancy occurred at St Peter's, butler with two men under him in the house of a retired ambassador. He was tall, spare, grave, and dignified. He looked, if not like a duke, at least like an actor of the old school who specialized in dukes' parts. He had tact, firmness, and self-assurance. His character was unimpeachable.

The vicar began briskly.

'Foreman, we've got something rather unpleasant to say to you. You've been here a great many years and I think his

87

lordship and the general agree with me that you've fulfilled the duties of your office to the satisfaction of everybody concerned.'

The two churchwardens nodded.

'But a most extraordinary circumstance came to my knowledge the other day and I felt it my duty to impart it to the churchwardens. I discovered to my astonishment that you could neither read nor write.'

The verger's face betrayed no sign of embarrassment.

'The last vicar knew that, sir,' he replied. 'He said it didn't make no difference. He always said there was a great deal too much education in the world for 'is taste.'

'It's the most amazing thing I ever heard,' cried the general. 'Do you mean to say that you've been verger of this church for sixteen years and never learned to read or write?'

'I went into service when I was twelve, sir. The cook in the first place tried to teach me once, but I didn't seem to 'ave the knack for it, and then what with one thing and another I never seemed to 'ave the time. I've never really found the want of it. I think a lot of these young fellows waste a rare lot of time readin' when they might be doin' something useful.'

'But don't you want to know the news?' said the other churchwarden. 'Don't you ever want to write a letter?'

'No, me lord, I seem to manage very well without. And of late years now they've all these pictures in the papers I get to know what's goin' on pretty well. Me wife's quite a scholar and if I want to write a letter she writes it for me. It's not as if I was a bettin' man.'

The two churchwardens gave the vicar a troubled glance and then looked down at the table.

'Well, Foreman, I've talked the matter over with these gentlemen and they quite agree with me that the situation is impossible. At a church like St Peter's, Neville Square, we cannot have a verger who can neither read nor write.'

Albert Edward's thin, sallow face reddened and he moved uneasily on his feet, but he made no reply.

'Understand me, Foreman, I have no complaint to make against you. You do your work quite satisfactorily; I have the highest opinion both of your character and of your capacity; but we haven't the right to take the risk of some accident that might happen owing to your lamentable ignorance. It's a matter of prudence as well as of principle.'

'But couldn't you learn, Foreman?' asked the general.

'No, sir, I'm afraid I couldn't, not now. You see, I'm not as young as I was and if I couldn't seem able to get the letters in me 'ead when I was a nipper I don't think there's much chance of it now.'

'We don't want to be harsh with you, Foreman,' said the vicar. 'But the churchwardens and I have quite made up our minds. We'll give you three months and if at the end of that time you cannot read and write I'm afraid you'll have to go.'

Albert Edward had never liked the new vicar. He'd said from the beginning that they'd made a mistake when they gave him St Peter's. He wasn't the type of man they wanted with a classy congregation like that. And now he straightened himself a little. He knew his value and he wasn't going to allow himself to be put upon.

'I'm very sorry, sir, I'm afraid it's no good. I'm too old a dog to learn new tricks. I've lived a good many years without knowin' 'ow to read and write, and without wishin' to praise myself, self-praise is no recommendation, I don't mind sayin' I've done my duty in that state of life in which it 'as pleased a merciful providence to place me, and if I *could* learn now I don't know as I'd want to.'

'In that case, Foreman, I'm afraid you must go.'

'Yes, sir, I quite understand. I shall be 'appy to 'and in my resignation as soon as you've found somebody to take my place.'

But when Albert Edward with his usual politeness had closed

the church door behind the vicar and the two churchwardens he could not sustain the air of unruffled dignity with which he had borne the blow inflicted upon him and his lips quivered. He walked slowly back to the vestry and hung up on its proper peg his verger's gown. He sighed as he thought of all the grand funerals and smart weddings it had seen. He tidied everything up, put on his coat, and hat in hand walked down the aisle. He locked the church door behind him. He strolled across the square, but deep in his sad thoughts he did not take the street that led him home, where a nice strong cup of tea awaited him; he took the wrong turning. He walked slowly along. His heart was heavy. He did not know what he should do with himself. He did not fancy the notion of going back to domestic service; after being his own master for so many years, for the vicar and churchwardens could say what they liked, it was he that had run St Peter's, Neville Square, he could scarcely demean himself by accepting a situation. He had saved a tidy sum, but not enough to live on without doing something, and life seemed to cost more every year. He had never thought to be troubled with such questions. The vergers of St Peter's, like the popes of Rome, were there for life. He had often thought of the pleasant reference the vicar would make in his sermon at evensong the first Sunday after his death to the long and faithful service, and the exemplary character of their late verger, Albert Edward Foreman. He sighed deeply. Albert Edward was a non-smoker and a total abstainer, but with a certain latitude; that is to say he liked a glass of beer with his dinner and when he was tired he enjoyed a cigarette. It occurred to him now that one would comfort him and since he did not carry them he looked about him for a shop where he could buy a packet of Gold Flake. He did not at once see one and walked on a little. It was a long street, with all sorts of shops in it, but there was not a single one where you could buy cigarettes.

'That's strange,' said Albert Edward.

To make sure he walked right up the street again. No, there was no doubt about it. He stopped and looked reflectively up and down.

'I can't be the only man as walks along this street and wants a fag,' he said. 'I shouldn't wonder but what a fellow might do very well with a little shop here. Tobacco and sweets, you know.'

He gave a sudden start.

'That's an idea,' he said. 'Strange 'ow things come to you when you least expect it.'

He turned, walked home, and had his tea.

'You're very silent this afternoon, Albert,' his wife remarked.

'I'm thinkin',' he said.

He considered the matter from every point of view and next day he went along the street and by good luck found a little shop to let that looked as though it would exactly suit him. Twenty-four hours later he had taken it, and when a month after that he left St Peter's, Neville Square, for ever, Albert Edward Foreman set up in business as a tobacconist and newsagent. His wife said it was a dreadful come-down after being verger of St Peter's, but he answered that you had to move with the times, the church wasn't what it was, and 'enceforward he was going to render unto Caesar what was Caesar's. Albert Edward did very well. He did so well that in a year or so it struck him that he might take a second shop and put a manager in. He looked for another long street that hadn't got a tobacconist in it and when he found it, and a shop to let, took it and stocked it. This was a success too. Then it occurred to him that if he could run two he could run half a dozen, so he began walking about London, and whenever he found a long street that had no tobacconist and a shop to let he took it. In the course of ten years he had acquired no less than ten shops and he was making money hand over fist. He went round to all of them himself every Monday, collected the week's takings, and took them to the bank.

One morning when he was there paying in a bundle of notes and a heavy bag of silver the cashier told him that the manager would like to see him. He was shown into an office and the manager shook hands with him.

'Mr Foreman, I wanted to have a talk to you about the money you've got on deposit with us. D'you know exactly how much it is?'

'Not within a pound or two, sir; but I've got a pretty rough idea.'

'Apart from what you paid in this morning it's a little over thirty thousand pounds. That's a very large sum to have on deposit and I should have thought you'd do better to invest it.'

'I wouldn't want to take no risk, sir. I know it's safe in the bank.'

'You needn't have the least anxiety. We'll make you out a list of absolutely gilt-edged securities. They'll bring you in a better rate of interest than we can possibly afford to give you.'

A troubled look settled on Mr Foreman's distinguished face. 'I've never 'ad anything to do with stocks and shares and I'd 'ave to leave it all in your 'ands,' he said.

The manager smiled. 'We'll do everything. All you'll have to do next time you come in is just to sign the transfers.'

'I could do that all right,' said Albert uncertainly. 'But 'ow should I know what I was signin'?'

'I suppose you can read,' said the manager a trifle sharply.

Mr Foreman gave him a disarming smile.

'Well, sir, that's just it. I can't. I know it sounds funny-like, but there it is, I can't read or write, only me name, an' I only learnt to do that when I went into business.'

The manager was so surprised that he jumped up from his chair.

'That's the most extraordinary thing I ever heard.'

'You see, it's like this, sir, I never 'ad the opportunity until it was too late and then some'ow I wouldn't. I got obstinate-like.'

The manager stared at him as though he were a prehistoric monster.

'And do you mean to say that you've built up this important business and amassed a fortune of thirty thousand pounds without being able to read or write? Good God, man, what would you be now if you had been able to?'

'I can tell you that, sir,' said Mr Foreman, a little smile on his still aristocratic features. 'I'd be verger of St Peter's, Neville Square.'

FOR THE BEST IN PAPERBACKS, LOOK FOR THE

In every corner of the world, on every subject under the sun, Penguin represents quality and variety – the very best in publishing today.

For complete information about books available from Penguin – including Pelicans, Puffins, Peregrines and Penguin Classics – and how to order them, write to us at the appropriate address below. Please note that for copyright reasons the selection of books varies from country to country.

In the United Kingdom: For a complete list of books available from Penguin in the U.K., please write to *Dept E.P., Penguin Books Ltd, Harmondsworth, Middlesex, UB7 0DA*

In the United States: For a complete list of books available from Penguin in the U.S., please write to *Dept BA, Penguin, 299 Murray Hill Parkway, East Rutherford, New Jersey 07073*

In Canada: For a complete list of books available from Penguin in Canada, please write to *Penguin Books Canada Ltd, 2801 John Street, Markham, Ontario L3R 1B4*

In Australia: For a complete list of books available from Penguin in Australia, please write to the *Marketing Department, Penguin Books Australia Ltd, P.O. Box 257, Ringwood, Victoria 3134*

In New Zealand: For a complete list of books available from Penguin in New Zealand, please write to the *Marketing Department, Penguin Books (NZ) Ltd, Private Bag, Takapuna, Auckland 9*

In India: For a complete list of books available from Penguin, please write to *Penguin Overseas Ltd, 706 Eros Apartments, 56 Nehru Place, New Delhi, 110019*

In Holland: For a complete list of books available from Penguin in Holland, please write to *Penguin Books Nederland B.V., Postbus 195, NL–1380AD Weesp, Netherlands*

In Germany: For a complete list of books available from Penguin, please write to *Penguin Books Ltd, Friedrichstrasse 10 – 12, D–6000 Frankfurt Main 1, Federal Republic of Germany*

In Spain: For a complete list of books available from Penguin in Spain, please write to *Longman Penguin España, Calle San Nicolas 15, E–28013 Madrid, Spain*